THE FLAME

By

Patrick Corcoran

"A man has to fend and fettle for the best, and then trust in something

beyond himself… So I believe in the little flame between us. For me

now, it's the only thing in the world."

Lady Chatterley's Lover, D. H. Lawrence (1885-1930)

Chapter 1

1968

"Ti amo," Catrin Rossini said, when she opened the box containing the pearl necklace. Sean had used money from his holiday job to buy the pearls. It was one of their last evenings in Cardiff, before Catrin moved into her flat in London. Since her summer holiday in Rome Catrin had become more sophisticated and this evening looked stunning in her cream silk dress and tan leather shoes - medium heels, square at the toe. She deftly slid the pearls around her slender neck, then clicked the clasp shut with a firm squeeze of her fingers.

"I want to play you some music, Sean." She shot him a quick, dazzling smile.

"What have you got?"

Since Sean's last visit, Catrin's father had bought a brand new hi-fi player and Catrin had discovered Beethoven. That evening she played one of Beethoven's piano sonatas over and over again. It had moved her, and she had wanted Sean to be moved as she had been.

And then she had played Nat King Cole. Such sweet sadness. ...'Since you went away the days grow long - but I miss you most of all, my darling - when autumn leaves start to fall...'

Catrin's parents had taken themselves to bed early and Sean and Catrin had danced as if clamped together standing in the living room next to the black leather corner suite - afraid to relax their embrace for even a moment lest the other, suddenly ashamed, might pull away breaking the mood of romance and infinite possibility which engulfed them and which they wanted to prolong without reflection or pause to a consummation only dreamed of until then. Sean had heard girls liked having their ears kissed and he had acted upon this, tenderly and with wonder. Catrin had shifted her stance. Her body now languorous in his arms. Sean was helpless. A man plunging over Niagara Falls in a barrel. They had toppled together onto the leather suite, Sean landing half on top of Catrin. There had been some fierce, hard kisses; Sean conscious only of the persistent pressure of Catrin's parted lips and the delicate taste of sugared almonds. The memory of this evening had remained deep within him sustaining a hope that his dream of love's fulfillment with Catrin would one day come true.

Sean needs to see Catrin again. He is hitch-hiking from his digs in New Brighton to her flat in Hampstead. Time has passed by so quickly, but he is going to her. To see his love. To see Catrin again.

A few feet away - the Mersey. The tide, fast-ebbing into a troubled Irish Sea. Across the river - the lights of Liverpool, vivid as pearls on honey-brown skin. His first lift has got him as far as the Seacombe landing stage at Wallasey. It is dark and almost deserted. No sign of a ferry. No people, apart from one man. The man is swaying; his eyes are in shadow and his boots are caked in cement. A strange, choking sound is coming from deep in the man's throat. Sean decides not to approach him.

Suddenly, the stranger begins shaking his head from side to side as if trying to regain his senses, like a boxer on the ropes soaking up too many of his opponent's punches. He makes a move. Feints to the right. Ducks left. Dances, up on his toes. Fists held high, elbows low protecting his ribs.

Seconds tick away. The man crabs towards Sean. Then retreats. He peers intently in Sean's direction from six feet away, sizing him up, before moving in again with an Ali shuffle, very nimbly considering the weight of cement on his boots. Suddenly a fist flicks out like an ant-eater's tongue. Sean registers the draught of air passing his right ear. He can only hope the man will lose interest. In a boxing match the bell would ring at the end of each round. A bell is ringing far out in the estuary – only warning of sandbanks. Gradually, the man's strength seems to ebb away. He stumbles backwards towards the edge of the landing stage. The water below him pounds against the pontoons. If he falls into the river, Sean realizes, the man's cement-covered boots will drag him under the river's churn within seconds. He grasps him by the forearm. At any moment he expects to be head-butted or punched but the man is docile now and looks at Sean as if wondering why he has gripped his arm.

Sean tries speaking as if nothing has happened.

"Excuse me, mate. I need a bit of help..."

The man appears not to have heard.

Sean tries again.

"I really need some help, pal. I'm hitching-hiking to London and a bloke in the pub said the East Lancs Road would be the quickest way to get to the M6…"

'Pal'. After four months living on The Wirral Peninsula Sean is losing his Cardiff accent.

He had chosen digs in New Brighton across the water from Liverpool because it had reminded him of visits to Barry Island as a child; day trippers, candy floss, the smell of chips - when the sun shone, lobster-burned shoulders everywhere you turned. During the autumn months, he discovered, New Brighton was very quiet - tumbleweed chip papers rolling along the streets and amusement arcades with flashing lights and very few people; but he liked living in New Brighton. It made no demands on him. He felt free.

"...Please, pal! I'm going to London... hitch-hiking. I want the East Lancs Road, and the motorway, the M6... Do you know how I can find them?"

"It's a long way tha'... London."

Sean manoeuvres himself and the man away from the pontoon's edge. The man taps his forehead, forcing his brain into action. At last he finds the words he needs.

"It's the East Lancs, you need... t'East Lancs Road. Over the water... Over there." The man waves his arm in a wide arc.

"There? By those glittering lights?"

"Yeh. Over there..." The man looks up, trying to decide whether or not Sean is making fun of him. He looks closely at Sean's brown cords, his brogues and tweed jacket, as if taking a dislike to them.

" 'Course this is the way to the friggin East Lancs. I'm trying to tell you... But the last bus will've gone..."

Sean's heart sinks like a stone. As if wanting to lessen Sean's disappointment, the man adds.

"...On the other side, like."

"And... the ferries? Are they still running?"

"The last one'll be over now, shortly.."

"Hey, thanks."

Sean's world is bearable again.

The man leans against him heavily. Looks fondly at him, as if Sean has been making a fuss about nothing.

"No other worries, 'ave you son?"

"Well... I'm hitch-hiking to see my girlfriend..."

"Ah! Woman troubles?..."

The man's head has stopped shaking. He leans on Sean even more heavily. The landing stage's pontoons are groaning beneath their feet.

"You are alright... you. You!... you're young...you'll be fine!"

The man's last speech takes a lot out of him. His eyes glaze over.

The lights of an approaching ferry pierce the darkness.

"Thanks... You're alright, too...."

Sean gently disengages himself from the man's embrace. The man's head starts shaking again. He sways to his right. Tries a left jab. Follows with a teasing uppercut which whistles through the air within an inch of Sean's chin.

Chapter 2

The ferry bumps across the Mersey. Sean feels much happier. He is on his way.

The man he met at the landing stage is also on the ferry and has followed him to the upper deck. Silence between them now. Time for a stiffener. Sean forages for his hip-flask in the bulging pockets of his tweed jacket.

Sean's mother, Noreen, had gone with him to buy the tweed jacket in a Cardiff department store. "You'll need something smart to go away to college, Sean," she had said.

Sean would have preferred the jacket not to have green elbow patches.

"It will wear better with those," his mother had said.

He would have liked ordinary buttons, too - not leather footballs. They came loose straightaway. Much to his relief. Were lost. Except for one, on the end of his left sleeve.

Still, his jacket is warm, it fits well, and he knows Noreen did not want him to feel at a disadvantage when mixing with the other law students. In its pockets he keeps his door key, lighter, cigarettes, comb, a clean handkerchief and his hip-flask given to him by his father, Cecil.

The hip-flask bears a Latin inscription. 'Amor Vincit Omnia'. Sean persuaded Cecil to have it done. He did not know what the best translation should be - 'Love Conquers All' perhaps; but he loved the seductive way Catrin pronounced the Latin words. "Amor...", she said it like the French word l'amour; "Vincit...", almost hissing between her teeth; "Omnia...", spoken slowly, softly, as if in a trance.

Sean had found the phrase in Chaucer's Canterbury Tales. The prioress had it on her brooch. Amor Vincit Omnia. Sean thought of it as one of Chaucer's jokes. Love. Carnality. Forbidden to clerics. What was it doing in this description of a convent prioress? Sean had read on. He came across The Wife of Bath and marvelled at her appetite for life. Five husbands. Not to mention 'other compaigny in youthe'. Sean was reassured. No matter how hopeless things seem. Love is around. Somewhere. Somehow. Sometime.

Chaucer was virtually the only erotic literature Sean had read but he represented a kind of lifeline. An earthy giver of hope. Sean wondered how Chaucer would write about him. An eighteen year old scholar. In this year of

Our Lord, nineteen sixty eight. Everybody seemingly making love not war. Except Sean. Lady Chatterley's Lover unread. A novel 'depraved and corrupting', according to the newspaper accounts. Just the place where Sean felt he might start to learn about life, other people's experiences, and what love is all about. The only copy of a D. H. Lawrence book he had found in the school library was Sea and Sardinia. Sean studied every page minutely. It was all about Lawrence and his 'Queen Bee', Frieda, trekking through the mountains - sampling life in rural Sardinia. There was nothing about love.

Yet something from Sea and Sardinia drifts back to him as the ferry approaches Pier Head, '...dark under the great carob tree as we go down the steps. Dark still the garden. Scent of mimosa, and then of jasmine.' Sean has a fleeting vision of Catrin. 'The lovely mimosa tree invisible. Dark the stony path.'

Sean offers his companion a sip from his hip-flask. It contains an amber nectar. Jameson's whisky. The man drinks long and hard. Sean also takes a mouthful. No more. He has a long journey ahead of him.

From the ferry's upper deck they watch as the ferry draws closer to the buildings lining the waterfront at the heart of the city, so heavily bombed in the Second World War yet never crushed and now rising again from the ashes.

Dominating the scene the twin towers of the Liver Building – Liverpool's

cornuto of defiance to the world at large.

Chapter 3

Sean remembers his father, Cecil, presenting him with the hip-flask. On his eighteenth birthday. A little ceremony.

"Here, son."

"Father?"

Cecil asks Sean to enter the room which he always refers to as his study. It is where the family meet to discuss serious matters. Sean's mother is already there.

"Have a seat, son."

Cecil is a self-contained man. He finds it hard to call Sean by his first name except on rare occasions and on those occasions its use sounds awkward to Sean's ears. Sean has grown up finding it more natural to refer to his father as 'Father' rather than 'Dad' or 'Cecil'.

The clock on the mantle-piece ticks loudly. It was presented to Cecil's father when he retired from the post office.

In front of Cecil, on the heat resistant table cover, is a small cardboard box. Someone has wiped the top and sides. A grimy duster lies in a heap, an arm's length from Cecil's right hand. His hand rests on the cardboard box. Sean notices that his father's fingers are trembling.

"This is for you, son..."

"Hey, thanks, father."

"...From your grandfather. That is... my father, Pop Connolly."

The flask is silver-plated, empty, but in mint condition.

Pop Connolly had died on the evening of his second marriage to a lovely widow, Mrs O'Brien, eleven years before. Sean still remembers her as Mrs O'Brien, not Mrs Connolly, her marriage to Pop Connolly having been so short. The flask had been a wedding present from Pop Connolly's friend, the local postmaster. After Pop died, Mrs O'Brien gave the flask to Cecil. Cecil had not liked the flask, associating it with what he considered to be Pop Connolly's over-fondness for whiskey and with alcohol in general. He had accepted it, Sean believed, only out of politeness. Yet Sean now notices that letting it go is a wrench for Cecil as he looks at Sean, his expression uncertain, vulnerable, almost pleading, and Sean senses that this flask means something for each of them, symbolizing their connection as father and son, sharing the same flesh and blood, both part of a line stretching back to the dawn of humanity. Nothing is said but Sean feels that at some level an understanding between himself and his father is just beginning, an understanding which neither of them can put into words or fully comprehend.

"He'd have wanted you to have something, son. Something to remember him by. I was going to keep it until you were twenty one. Mother thought you should have it now. Do you want to keep it in the box?"

"No, I don't think so, father. I'll pop it straight in my pocket, thanks."

"As you wish."

"Thank you, I will treasure it."

The hip-flask always reminds Sean of Pop Connolly. Some happy memories. Some sad. Pop Connolly had been living with Cecil, Noreen and Sean until his sudden death on the first night of his marriage to Mrs O'Brien and so his funeral took place in Cardiff. Sean was an altar server. He remembers Father Columbus squeezing between Pop Connolly's coffin and the front benches in the church to sprinkle holy water on the coffin. Sean was carrying the holy water bucket. Father Columbus had sprinkled water far and wide. Cold drops of water had landed on Sean's hair, his face, his cheeks. He wiped them away with the sleeve of his surplice. He did not want his family and their friends to think he was crying. Pop Connolly would be going to heaven and he had been told they should rejoice for him.

Back at the house, after the burial, Sean hears Mrs O'Brien talking to his mother.

"...Sad, yes, Noreen, that he died on our wedding night. A tragedy, yet a great blessing too...in a way."

Noreen looks shocked. Mrs O'Brien has never looked calmer.

"He died so happy, you see. Ah, yes. Someone in Heaven was looking after him that night."

Noreen would have preferred to end the conversation there but Sean can see Mrs O'Brien is not finished.

"He died... how can I put it? That's it... he died with a smile on his face, Noreen. And who could wish for more than that? Just one tumbler of Jameson's he had for a nightcap, before retiring to bed."

"Despite the diabetes, Mrs O'Brien?"

"I could'nt deprive him, Noreen. Not on his wedding night. Down the hatch it went... Connolly's digestion was always on the delicate side, wasn't it? Yet little did I realize at that moment what was to come..."

The family draws closer around Mrs O'Brien. Interested.

"First, Connolly gets into bed in his socks, frisky as a new born lamb and with a twinkle in his eye he says, 'What I could do with now, Mrs O'Brien...' Says I, 'Call me Mrs Connolly, please, mister. We're married now, you know.' He laughed until he went blue in the face. Then, 'Mrs

Connolly,' says he squeezing my hand, 'What I could do with now is a tasty little... succulent bit of... soda water!' Then he started laughing again, fit to bust."

"Poor Pop," says Noreen.

"He'd such a sense of humour, hadn't he, Noreen? 'Just a drop of soda water... to round off a perfect day, Mrs O'Br... Mrs Connolly.' "

"He didn't know when to stop… was his problem," says Noreen.

"Ah, well, God is merciful, though," Mrs O'Brien retorts, "Anyway, I got meself up out of bed to fetch the soda water. 'Oh,' he says. Surprised like. I kneel down beside him. 'Oh,' he says again. And... and, he looks up at me with that little smile on his face..."

Mrs O'Brien pauses to dab her eyes with a fresh Kleenex.

"And, then... he just drifted away. Thinking of quenching his thirst with soda water. Clutching my hand for all he was worth, right to the end."

"Poor Pop," repeats Noreen, stoically.

"I dabbed a few drops of Jameson's on his lips right away, trying to revive him, but he had already gone."

"God rest his soul," says Cecil.

Noreen launches into the usual prayer for the dead.

"Eternal rest grant unto him, Oh Lord. And let perpetual light shine upon him. May he rest in peace. Amen."

When the prayers started up Mrs O'Brien went home and Sean rarely saw her after that.

Pop Connolly was buried with his first wife, Mammy Connolly, in Ely Cemetery, Cardiff. He and Mammy had come to live with Cecil and Noreen because of Pop's health. He missed Ireland and used to regale Sean with tales of his Irish childhood like someone reliving a dream. Then, as a young man, he had joined the British Army, and had never returned to County Carlow where he was born, nor to Ireland - something which Sean did not understand. At the graveside Sean noticed one old lady dressed all in black standing apart from the rest of the mourners. Later, Cecil told him the lady had grown up in Bagenalstown, the village in Ireland where Pop Connolly was born. She was clutching a little branch of weeping willow. Sean saw her throw it gently towards Pop Connolly's coffin as it was lowered into the grave. Cecil said he was told that she had brought it with her from the farm where she grew up. The willow branch landed on the far side of the grave where Father Columbus was standing on the freshly dug clay reading out prayers for the repose of Pop Connolly's soul. The leaves of the weeping willow got caught up in the hem of Father Columbus's cassock. Back in the sacristy, he finally noticed it.

"God, look at my cassock and the state of my boots, Sean," he said.

"I've brought half the cemetery back with me."

He plucked the weeping willow branch off his cassock and dropped it into a waste bin along with several lumps of mud from his boots.

What made Sean sad was that his grandfather's brother, old Declan Connolly, from his farm in Ireland, could not make it. Pop Connolly had talked so much about him and had promised to take Sean to Ireland one day to meet him. But Sean and Pop Connolly never made the trip. It became one of Pop Connolly's unfulfilled wishes.

"Here's to the fine men of Ireland, Sean... and not forgetting the rest of us!" He would wink. Chin held high. Tramlines of skin quivering in his neck. The memory of his voice drifts back to Sean, stays with him, like the soothing drone of a bumblebee on a hot summer's afternoon.

"Study your history well, Sean - your Prime Ministers; Sir Robert Walpole, Willy Pitt 'The Elder' and 1st Earl of Chatham who was the Prime Minister from 1766 until 1768, and all the rest of them, Willy Pitt 'The Younger', Sir Robert Peel, Viscount Palmerston, Benjamin Disraeli, Willy Gladstone, Sir Henry Campbell-Bannerman, Davy Lloyd-George. All great men with grand names, grand names, don't you think? And never neglect the Kings and Queens of England, Sean. They are the most important of all. Knowing about them and the dates they reigned can only set yous in good stead."

Sean knew that Pop Connolly had a great respect for languages, learning, academic achievement.

"Yes, grandad," he would reply, feeling too hot in front of his grandfather's electric fire. The sun blazing outside. Wanting to go over to Clarence Park to play football with his friend, Patrick Delaney.

Chapter 4

Noreen and Cecil share Pop Connolly's passion for education.

"Right, Sean. Which subjects are you going to study at Advanced Level?" Cecil and Noreen are talking to Sean in Cecil's study.

"You need to bear in mind the career you intend to follow when you make your choice, son."

Cecil's expression is one of kindly concern. Noreen is nodding in support of Cecil.

Sean already knew his father wanted him to be a solicitor and that his mother felt certain he would make an excellent teacher. Why his father's view prevailed, he never fully understood.

"Latin, French and English are a must for people intending to study law," Cecil says. Sean wants to do Art, Music and anything else not involving too much remembering of facts.

"People can do Art and Music as hobbies..." Cecil cajoles. Noreen nods again as if sympathizing with Sean over the fact that the die tends to be cast once Cecil makes up his mind.

Sean does not blame Noreen and Cecil for guiding him. He has no idea what he wants. He would love to live in a camper-van by the sea or, even better, work as a beach lifeguard in Biarritz? Outdoor work appeals to him. Bricklaying would be perfect. He imagines having big muscles would give him confidence to walk tall in the world without needing to look over his shoulder to check he was safe and would enable him to build garages for friends in his spare time, and be the sort of friend who was both good company and handy, able to do others a favour and always be welcomed in their homes. Lumber-jacking in Canada or sheep farming in Australia might well fit the bill but he cannot bring himself to leave school and explore the world. He is trapped by loyalty to his parents, obedience to their wishes, and what people keep calling the need to achieve his 'full potential'.

When Sean gets his Advanced Level examination results he is on a ferry in the Bay of Biscay. Southampton-bound on the SS Santander.

He has been on a pilgrimage organized by Cecil to the shrine of Our Lady Of Fatima in Portugal. Sean has prayed there for success in his exams but Our Lady Of Fatima has not yet given Sean any sign that she is going to work any miracles to help. Sean is not really surprised. He realizes Our Lady of Fatima may be busy responding to more important requests. Nonetheless, he cannot help hoping that she will at least consider his pilgrimage to be worth making sure his grades are all B's, to guarantee his entry to university in London.

Sean's belief in God's willingness to intervene in his life has fluctuated. An early example was the day of his first Holy Communion. Sean was very excited at the prospect of being allowed to take Holy Communion each Sunday like his parents and all the other grown-ups.

At the appointed time he processed towards the altar rail with all the other children in single file; the girls in white frocks, white gloves and white veils, the boys in white shirts, white flannel trousers and white plimsolls. Half way down the aisle disaster struck.

It was Brendan Chigley who inadvertently shattered Sean's world by treading heavily on the heel of Sean's left plimsoll causing it to come off. Brendan was walking directly behind Sean with eyes closed and deep in prayer. Sean could hear him reciting last minute Acts of Contrition.

"Oh, my God, I am sorry I have sinned against Thee - say but the word and my soul shall be healed... Please, please, God."

It had been impressed upon them that their souls must be pure when they received their First Communion. They had to be in 'a state of grace'. If they committed bad sins before taking communion they would be sure to burn in hell for all eternity. Sean could not help wondering what sins Brendan had committed which had resulted in him making frantic last minute Acts of Contrition, but he continued walking ahead slowly and reverently, in the manner in which they had been taught. He just managed to hang on to his plimsoll by shoving his foot back into the front part. He would have liked to crouch down to pull it back on properly but it was not possible. He could not stop. He was too near the altar rail and the priest would have wondered what he was doing. He approached the altar rail sliding his left foot along the ground, like a skier on one ski. Not as respectful of God's presence as he should have been. To anybody who did not understand the situation he looked as if he didn't want to be there at all as he slouched along to ensure continuing contact between his foot and the plimsoll, literally dragging his feet, or more accurately, foot. God did nothing to help him in his hour of need, when he and God were about to meet in the Holy Sacrament of the Eucharist for the first time. There was a disappointing absence of supernatural intervention which Sean ultimately put down to his own unworthiness.

Sean knew that faith in God's existence was essential to be a good Catholic boy. His prayers were not answered in the way he desired but 'Faith' surrounded him on all sides, at home, at school and all around the many

Catholic parishes throughout Cardiff. Nearly all the people he knows have 'The Faith'. Sean pictures them and himself as God's knights, clanking through their lives in Faith Suits Of Armour trying as hard as possible to be good, kind and loving. That is all he wants too. He knows they all play by the same rules. They are modest. Humble. In awe of priestly guidance and authority. All safely strapped inside Faith Suits Of Armour worshipping their king, Jesus.

Sean can look back on years of trying to be good. It started when he was young in Saint Boniface's. His first religious experiences were at floor level, scrambling down from his mother's arms, straddling the heating pipes which ran parallel to the kneelers, staring at the legs of the people in the bench in front. Brown sandals; pretty ankle socks with lace around their edge; shiney-sharp stiletto heels; shapely calves in black-seamed nylons; crepe brothel creepers; fluorescent green socks. Peering into the mysterious shadows, higher up. Turning around. Gazing up the noses of the adults in the bench behind. Smiling at their children – "Mummy, why is that little boy looking at us?" Sean is told to, "Face the front, Sean! Good… good… that's a good boy." He sits up straight on the bench facing forward, concentrating on his pearly prayer book and playing with his first set of Rosary Beads which contain, in the hollow crucifix, a tiny fragment of mud from the catacombs in

Rome, where the bones of the early Christian saints are buried .

Sean is praised even more when he starts to follow the Mass in his big boy's Latin Missal. Cecil pats the top of his head, "That's good, Sean. Very good. Very clever."

Not only has Sean completed the pilgrimage to Our Lady Of Fatima's shrine in Portugal, he has done penance there, standing for hours on a vast piazza, praying with thousands of other pilgrims in the blazing sun. Sean has offered it all up for his sins as well as praying that he will do well in his exams. He has tried hard to avoid sinful temptation despite being bowled over by the beauty of the manager of the pensione where he and the other pilgrims stay. He knows that 'looking' is a sin if it gives rise to sinful thoughts. He averts his gaze from Olivinha's rounded lips, smooth and full like tangerine segments, and looks at her only when greeting her at breakfast and wishing her a good night.

Sean's exam results come through at breakfast time on the S.S. Santander. Seamus, his cousin, had agreed to check the post and contact him as soon as the letter arrived. Sean hears an announcement on the ship's loudspeaker system.

"A call for Mister Sean Connolly. Mister Sean Connolly to the radio telephone operator's cabin, please."

The SS Santander is pitching a bit. The other pilgrims, those well enough, look up and smile at him. Sean's parents give him the thumbs up sign.

As expected, it is Seamus calling on the ship's radio telephone.

"Seamus here... Over." A stickler for correct procedure, Seamus.

"G... C... E... Advanced Level examination results follow."

"Come on Seamus, hurry up."

"Are you ready to receive?... Over."

Sean is grateful to Seamus. He is desperate to know whether he will be going to Kings College, London, to read Law and live near Catrin. He waits impatiently for Seamus to get to the point. He dwells on his usual outlandish fantasies of life after qualifying as a lawyer - copious portions of caviar, champagne, a Ferrari, the best seats in theatres and Catrin dripping with pearls, pearls and more pearls; pearl bracelets, pearl nightgowns, pearl tiaras, pearl bikinis at Ostia - Catrin in pearls for ever!

"Your results are as follows, Sean... Over."

"Oh my God… Our Lady Of Fatima, pray for me. Please let me pass with at least three B's…"

"English, B for Bravo... French, B for Bravo... Latin E for Echo... That completes the message... Over and out."

As Sean wanders back along the deck of the S.S. Santander preparing to tell Cecil and Noreen that he has only achieved an E for Echo in Latin, he ponders on what more he could have done. Has he not been devout enough? Not prayed hard enough? He chides himself for agreeing to study Latin in the first place. Cecil had talked him into it and Sean just did not have his father's or Pop Connolly's passion for Latin translation or for learning in general.

He stares resignedly across the Bay of Biscay at the vastness of the Atlantic Ocean. So studying law at King's College, London, is not to be. But he determines Catrin shall have her pearls. A few weeks later, he has secured a place to study law - it will be an external law degree at Liverpool's College of Commerce in Tithebarn Street - his new passport to lawyership and riches.

Chapter 5

The Mersey ferry has come alongside at Pier Head, Liverpool. Sean's friend points him in the direction of the East Lancs Road.

Then, suddenly, "Driscoll…" He whispers his name into Sean's ear. As if it is a closely guarded secret. "…And may your God go with you."

They shake hands.

"It's been a pleasure meeting you, Mr Driscoll."

Sean leaves Driscoll standing on the landing stage at Pier Head. He is staring back. Staring at the lights flickering across the water at Seacombe. At the place from which they have just travelled.

Chapter 6

In London, earlier that evening, Catrin has returned from work with her flat-mate, Penny. They work as typists for the BBC World Service in Bush House - Catrin for the Italian section under the firm guidance of Signora Debove, and Penny with the international news department.

Their flat on Haverstock Hill, Hampstead, is near Belsize Park Tube Station. Catrin often enjoys walking up to Hampstead Heath after the rush-hour crush on the tube. She finds this burns off the energy which builds up whilst sitting at her typewriter all day.

Since coming to London Catrin has thought a lot about Sean; how his A level results meant he could not study law at Kings College as he had intended and instead had found a law degree course in Liverpool. She thinks about him every day and writes to him at least three times a week.

Catrin's flat is on the ground floor of a spacious semi-detached villa. She and Penny can only afford the rent with a lot of help from their parents but it suits their needs perfectly. In their living room there are astrakhan rugs covering the floor and plush sofas to sink into. There is a spacious bathroom, a well-equipped kitchen, and one other room which they use as a shared bedroom. The ceilings are high with ornate plaster moldings, the most notable of which is a ceiling rose which forms a centre-piece in the living room. They could so easily have fitted Sean in on one of the couches in the living room, Catrin reflects sadly.

When she first moved to London Catrin had been based in a girls' hostel in Shaftesbury Avenue run by Roman Catholic nuns. Her life had been regulated by a strict 'in-by-ten-o'clock' curfew and non-residents were not allowed in except to attend Sunday Mass in the hostel chapel. She and Penny had found the flat in Hampstead through Penny's boss at the BBC. Once there Catrin's horizons had broadened in unexpected ways. One morning she had been gathering their bottles of milk from their doorstep when she encountered the postman. He had told her in a whisper that a Mr Huxley lived in the basement flat, right beneath them, in the very same building as themselves.

"A nice gentleman he is, belongs to the famous Huxley family, I believe. Don't tell anyone I told you but I have only ever seen him in his dressing gown..."

When Catrin told Penny this, Penny was deeply impressed. She knew somebody called Huxley had written "Brave New World". Penny said her brother had done an essay about "Brave New World" at school. She was pretty sure Aldous Huxley was the author. "But I think I read that Aldous Huxley passed away a few years ago, so it probably isn't him living downstairs." Despite this, Catrin and Penny felt sure their neighbour must be someone special and invariably referred to him as… "Our Mr Huxley" despite the mystery over his identity and the fact that they had never seen, met, or spoken to him.

Living in London has been a revelation for Catrin. There is so much to see and so many interesting people. She often sees faces in the lift at Bush House previously only seen on her TV screen. On all sides she finds herself surrounded by rich, successful people. She keeps up appearances by being very careful how she spends her salary so that every month she has some money left over. Her favourite treat is buying new clothes.

Pouring out cups of tea for herself and Penny, Catrin is telling Penny all about her day.

"I sprinted up to Carnaby Street during my lunch hour – bought a dress in Lady Jane's and some kinky boots in Topper's. Do you want to see?" Penny fondles the pink floral miniskirt and inspects the white lace-up boots admiringly.

"Wow! It's a kind of velvet, the skirt! Absolutely fab!" Penny exclaims. "You'll look like Sophia Loren in that."

Catrin continues, "Old Ma Debove wasn't too happy when I got back to the office. 'This IS the BBC, you know, Miss Rossini,' she said… 'I trust you won't be wearing those things to work here…' She thinks skirts should go no higher than the ankle and curses in Italian when she sees what I buy!"

Catrin goes into the bedroom to try on her new clothes. She promises herself she will share her new coffee with Penny later, before they go out, if they do go out later. She has bought some coffee so they can make real espressos whenever they fancy one.

She closes the bedroom curtains and puts on a disc by her favourite Italian singer, Gianni Morandi, "Ma quando si fa sera….". The urgency of his voice makes her feel romantic. She tries on her new dress and the white boots. They make her feel special. She dances slowly around the bedroom in the dark. She is thinking of Sean in the way she used to think of him during the summer when she was lying on the beach in the sunshine at Ostia wishing he was there with her. The memory is mixed. It brings back her sense of irritation over an older boy, Augusto, who had pestered her, kept showing off, wanting to speak English with her all the time. He had always jumped into the seat next to her on the bus. She did not like his wispy moustache or the way he put his hand on her thigh without asking. They were with a group of families who travelled to the beach together each day. Catrin was staying with her Uncle Bruno's family in Rome and in the end she had asked Uncle Bruno to do something because she already had a boyfriend in Wales and Augusto was bothering her. Uncle Bruno had spoken to Augusto's father but, although Augusto then stopped bothering her he had spent the rest of the holiday scowling at Catrin from a distance whenever they were at the beach, which had been almost worse than when he had been pestering her all the time. It still irked Catrin. Why, she asked herself, did boys and men always assume you wanted their attention when you just wanted to mind your own business?

Catrin switches on the bedroom light and studies her reflection in the mirror. If he had been here, Sean could have said, "Che bella", with his best Cardiff pronunciation, she reflects. She has taught him some Italian phrases because he likes the sound of the Italian language so much.

She returns to the living room. "Are we going out tonight, Penny? I'd like to give my new clothes a whirl!"

Penny has a part time job as a cinema usherette at the cinema just up the road and is due to work there this evening. She gets free tickets to give to friends. Catrin has seen Ben Hur twice already but she has nowhere else to go this evening.

"Let's go," she says, "We can wash up the tea things when we get back…"

Before they leave the flat Catrin and Penny are in stitches. They have a real hoot. Penny dresses in her usherette uniform ready for work and, switching off all the lights in the flat, she shines the piercing beam of her usherette's torch in all directions. She aims the torch's beam at Catrin's feet shouting, "Mind the step… mind the step", as she herself stumbles down imaginary steps in the living room, throwing herself to the floor, laughing and spluttering, "I said mind the step, didn't I?" And then she pretends to patrol the back seats of the cinema, officiously shining her torch into the faces of customers whom she accuses of misbehaving, "Would you be kind enough to behave… Please!! We can't have that sort of behaviour here… I am afraid I'm going to have to call the manager…" Penny has performed this routine before. It never fails to amuse them.

On their return home they chat for a while about how boring Ben Hur was and, because Penny's boyfriend is coming to sleep over later in the week, they discuss what food they will buy in to make him feel welcome. They always plan ahead when they have any visitors to stay. They find it works better that way. They drink their espressos watching T.V. and then take themselves to bed.

Catrin is lying in bed thinking about the cinema trip to the Haverstock Hill Odeon earlier in the evening. She cannot sleep. She has had trouble sleeping ever since coming to London. At first it was straightforward home sickness. Now it is harder to put her finger on it. It is dark in the bedroom. The espresso has probably not helped though she can already hear her friend breathing deeply, fast asleep.

Catrin pulls her winceyette sheet tightly around her neck and shoulders. The weight of her blankets is just right. It is not cold but she still cannot sleep. Tonight she is thinking of home.

She misses her parents, she is all they have, and she misses her big black Labrador, Nicky, almost as much as she misses her parents whom she telephones every day. But telephoning, she knows, cannot compare with seeing them. Her father, Ted, has doted on her since she arrived in the world six days early, in 1949. His eyes had locked on her enormous dark eyes, her tiny hands, her quiff of black hair and he had been smitten. He was as much in love with Catrin as he was with Catrin's mother, Maria. This was apparent to all who knew him. His heart was so full of love he was unable to distinguish his love for the one from his love for the other and experienced unadulterated overflowing happiness whenever he was with them. Catrin knew how much they were both missing her. The phrase she used to console herself, although it did not ease the pain totally, was - at least they still have each other.

Her parents had been destined for each other ever since their first meeting in Rome. It was during the Second World War. Ted was a British soldier, part of the British and American Allied force which pushed up Italy from Sicily. Maria was a beautiful young woman living with her family in Rome. Catrin's parents' story had sounded so romantic and their love for each other was so deep that Catrin thought of herself as having been created out of pure love.

Once her parents met, their one desire had been for the war to end so that they could settle down together. When it ended they had married in Rome, in dazzling sunshine. Ted had persuaded Maria's father to let her move with him to Cardiff, and he had set himself up in business, in a small bicycle shop.

Cycling had been very popular after the Second World War and the shop had done well, well enough to allow Ted to indulge his passion for all things American. He bought a Chevrolet Impala which was the talk of Cardiff. Ted loved driving up in the car and parking outside their bicycle shop. It probably brought in more business than any amount of advertising would have done. Its bodywork was a dazzling red, its tyre walls were as white as freshly-fallen snow, and its broad tailfins extended as wide as the wings of any giant bird of prey.

Catrin smiles to herself recalling how Sean had once washed and polished Ted's Chevrolet on a Saturday, when Sean could have been doing any number of things elsewhere. Ted had fully accepted Sean after that as a member of his small, tight-knit family. It had been as if Ted had been checking Sean's suitability to be with his daughter, by the one test of character he really believed in – whether or not Sean would wash and polish the Chevrolet to a high enough standard. Catrin had liked that Sean and her father accepted each other, and she liked Sean for giving up his Saturday to do this chore for her father. She felt it showed he cared about her too. It made her feel safe and secure.

She and Sean had been so happy when she was living at home in Cardiff. She has so many memories of that time which often come back to her when she is trying to get to sleep. There was that day when her father had driven her and Sean into town in the Chevrolet Impala to see The

Beatles concert. The show was in The Capitol. As her father drove nearer and nearer the venue lots of fans had crowded around the car, looking in, wondering who they were, wondering if they were The Beatles. It had been so thrilling. She had felt like a famous pop star herself! She had not known Sean long but she had wanted to see The Beatles with a boy rather than with a group of girlfriends; and they had been in great seats. They could see John, Paul, George and Ringo perfectly, although they heard hardly any of the music because of the incessant screaming all around them.

Catrin had feared Sean might feel out of place. There were so many girls there. But he had paid no attention to them and had held her hand all the way through the show. He had kissed her suddenly and quickly on her cheek while Paul was singing 'Yesterday'. It had been amazing. She had known Sean was going to kiss her just before he did it. Somehow she had known he was going to choose that very moment. That was when she felt sure that they were really well suited. They had kept holding hands after the show too, standing on the pavement in Queen Street among the jostling crowds of fans, waiting for her father to pick them up.

She begins to feel drowsy. Half awake. Half asleep. She turns over. The hum of traffic on Haverstock Hill reminds her she is in a city which never sleeps.

Her thoughts drift to the magical time she and Sean had last Christmas in Cardiff. After Midnight Mass. She had persuaded Sean back to her parents' house to exchange presents. There had been just Catrin and her parents there, in their flat above the bicycle shop.

She and Sean had sat close together on the black leather corner suite in the living room. Her mother had started things off handing a square, flat package to her father. He, embarrassed that they were all watching, had made awkward small talk while wrestling with the wrapping paper and Sellotape, all the while glancing shyly at Catrin's mother.

"It feels interesting. What can it be, I wonder?"

He had tried to look puzzled even though Catrin was sure he had guessed what was inside. Then, finally, a look of delight had spread across his face.

"Aha!.. that record I've been wanting for ages… Frank Sinatra. Perfect!"

"That was the one, wasn't it?" her mother had beamed.

Sean had smiled gallantly throughout the family's present-giving and made a real effort to fit in. The only problem had been that he only had one present with him, which he had planned to give to Catrin after Midnight Mass. He had not expected to be asked back to Catrin's home. Catrin had felt so sorry for him. Sean had brought her present along in a green plastic Marks and Spencer bag without any Christmas wrapping paper around it.

Her parents had given Catrin a pink dressing gown, fluffy and flowing, clearly spun in a fairy workshop from a hundred feather boas. She had given her father a red and white striped shirt and her mother a butterfly wing brooch which she had immediately pinned on her mother's cardigan. The present of the night was her father's gift to her mother of diamond earrings. The Christmas tree lights had caused the earrings to throw out sudden sparks of colour. Her mother had thrown her arms around her father in a passionate embrace. No words had been needed.

She remembers how her parents at one point had simultaneously taken sips from their glasses of sherry. They had laughed. "Snap," they had said. Then they had laughed again because they had said 'snap' at the same time too. Sean had chosen that moment to give Catrin her Christmas present from him. She had loved the pair of brown corduroy slippers he had given her not because they would match the fluffy pink dressing gown her parents had given her, they would not, but because Sean had taken the trouble to go into town to buy them for her. Catrin's parents had nodded in approval over the effort he had obviously made and, later on, when he had left the flat her mother had taken her aside and said, 'He's truly simpatico, Catrin. I like him'.

Catrin had wrapped her present for Sean in gold foil - a pewter tankard engraved with his initials and a card which read, 'For Sean. Christmas 1967. With Love, Catrin.'

"That's a brilliant present. Thanks a million, Catrin." Sean had been delighted. He had pretended to drink from the tankard and had then stood up and politely patted her on her back. He had not wanted to over-step the mark in front of her parents.

Her parents had improvised brilliantly so that Sean would not feel left out. They had given him two bottles of beer to go with the tankard, a box of amarettos and a box of mince pies.

Later, her parents had gone into the kitchen to wash the sherry glasses and Sean had taken the hint that it was time to leave. Catrin had shown Sean out through the bicycle shop downstairs where she had hugged him and given him a peck on the cheek. She had instantly been aware of his reaction, the warmth of his response. In his arms she had felt safe.

"Good night, Catrin."

"Good night, Sean."

After he had gone Catrin could not have been happier. Cardiff was the most perfect place in the universe to be at that moment.

Catrin moves between sleep and wakefulness. Finally, despite the hum of traffic on Haverstock Hill and the sound of the footsteps of passers-by on the pavement outside, Catrin sleeps.

Chapter 7

Sean's thumb is out. A Jaguar saloon stops. Its driver is revving the engine impatiently.

"Hop in, old boy. Where you off to?" A man in his early forties sporting a handle-bar moustache is staring intently into Sean's eyes.

"M6 motorway?"

"Bingo! I'll get you there in no time!"

The driver's eyes are bloodshot. Once Sean is seated he pulls off at speed and starts talking without introducing himself.

"Life's a bitch, isn't it? A focking bitch, don't you think so... er..?"

"Sean..."

"A focking bitch, Sean. Heart specialist today. Ticker trouble. When he had finished all the tests he gave it to me straight. No booze. No fags. No driving. No sex. I could go at any time, he said. New heart I need, like that focking South African fella had - but there is nothing like that over here."

Sean mumbles his commiserations.

"Not supposed to drive... me, an ex-Spitfire pilot. Battle of Britain.

Bloody heroes we were… and now this."

He drives the car as fast as a Spitfire. Nearly. Over ninety anyway.

"We read about the Battle of Britain, at school," Sean responds without thinking, then wishes he hadn't.

"Read about us, eh? In focking history."

"Modern history, it was."

"Really... young, what's your name again...?"

"Sean..."

"Young, Sean. Read about us, eh?"

To Sean's surprise, the ex-Spitfire pilot looks gratified for a moment as he smoothes the ends of his moustaches upward.

"But what is there left to live for? Eh? WHAT... IS... LEFT..?" He glares at Sean, as if Sean is the cause of his ticker trouble.

Sean moans inwardly. He has a lot to live for. And has not really started yet.

The driver's jaw muscles clench and unclench. A man of action doomed to taking things easy for the rest of his life.

"Perhaps you just need... some time. To think about things?"

"Think. THINK, chum. That's the last thing I want to do."

He presses hard on the throttle and lights a cigarette with shaking hands temporarily letting go of the steering wheel.

"Picked you up to talk. To take my mind off things. Not to think. Frightened I was going to top myself, back there..."

The man's despair is palpable and Sean can only feel deep sympathy for a man willing to risk his life on behalf of Sean's generation at a time when he was no older than Sean is now and he guesses he has probably been trying to make up time for what the war stole from him ever since. Sean keeps a respectful silence and hopes that having his company will help the man as they hurtle through the city streets towards the East Lancs Road. At least as a wartime hero the Spitfire pilot has lived, whatever he is experiencing now, Sean thinks. Probably cut quite a dash with the girls in those days in his RAF uniform, his cap at a jaunty angle, pilot's wings on his chest, living for the moment.

Sean realises that if the car crashes the ambulance crew in attendance will find nothing to help identify him; just a blood-stained hip-flask in his pocket engraved with the words Amor Vincit Omnia. "What sort of a name is that?" they will murmur in muted tones, and Cecil and Noreen will not know what has happened; his life will be over and forgotten about almost before it has started.

Sean spots some lights ahead. The town of St Helens. Through it dangerously fast. He makes a sincere Act of Contrition. The Catholic Church teaches that a person's sins will be absolved immediately if you pray for forgiveness when facing imminent death, without having to go to a priest to confess your sins… "Oh, my God! I am most heartily sorry for all my sins; and I detest them above all things, because they displease Thee, Who art infinitely good and amiable, and I firmly resolve, with the help of Thy grace, to do penance for them, and never more to offend Thee…"

Time stands still. Sean is gripped by an all-consuming fear like when some older children pushed him and his friend Patrick Delaney down an almost vertical slope so that, half running, half falling, their bodies completely out of control, they tumbled, almost flying, into the stinging nettles at the bottom of the slope.

St Helens is now just a blur in the nearside wing mirror and the car's speed distorts the scenery as it whizzes past.

Sean's life, though short, has had moments of great happiness, notably when he has been in love . Some of these encounters flash through his mind like a Mutoscope, while he recites his final Act of

Contrition and prays to his God, the Creator of All Life on Earth, with a humble and contrite heart.

First day in nursery school.

Emmy.

Saw Sean had nothing to play with.

Said, "Don't cry, Sean".

Went over to the toy box.

Found him a shiny, wooden jigsaw.

Angie, who lived next door.

Came in with her mother one day.

"I'm going to lend you a penny," Angie said.

Sean did not know what 'lend' meant.

He accepted the coin.

Later Angie said,

"Can I have my penny back now?"

Obediently, Sean returned the coin.

They became firm friends.

Another day, in the garden

Angie plucked a leaf from the hedge.

Folded it between her fingers.

Held the leaf near Sean's ear.

Sqeezed it.

Sean heard a squish.

"That's a man and a lady kissing," she said.

The girl in Llandaff Fields.

Sitting on the grass with her friend

Under the conker trees,

Their bikes lying on the grass nearby

Little pennants fluttering on the handlebars.

Sean, playing football nearby

Didn't have the nerve to speak to her.

On a train, Desiree, lovely wheat-coloured hair,

Slipped her Wiltshire address into Sean's pocket

When the nun she was travelling with wasn't looking.

They each wrote one letter

But never saw each other again.

Deidre at Fontygary

Her kisses making Sean dizzy.

Met that evening.

Only spent an hour and a half together,

Sean had been swimming in the sea and smoking Woodbines.

Deidre was crisp and fresh. Been eating cockles in vinegar.

Short and sweet.

Her holiday ended next day.

The girl without a name

Who let him have the last dance

In Llandaff Memorial Hall.

When he did not think she would.

A slow one.

The song went on for ever,

Neither spoke a word.

Tracey and her friends

At the lake,

Sean a working hand at the boat-stage

Helping customers into the rowing boats.

Tracey rowing wildly

Crashing into the ornamental lighthouse

Did Tracey care? She kept splashing her oars

The lighthouse was in her way.

Sean kept rescuing them

Towed them back.

Tracey came down to the boat-stage

Giggling

Every day for a week.

Sean knows he is out of his depth. Knows he puts girls on a pedestal. There are no girls at home. No girls in his school. He sees them on the bus going to and from school. He does not know them. He sees them in white veils in Church during the month of May which is dedicated to Jesus' mother, Mary. He sees statues in church of beautiful, devout women. He needs more time. Not to be dashed against the mahogany fascia of this Jaguar. He and Catrin just need time together. Life has still got a lot to offer. His journey is just beginning. One chance is all he asks, not be cut down in his prime.

"Tally-ho... Not far to the M6 now, old chap..."

"Could you drop me off along here, please?... ahhh."

Sean shuts his eyes as the Jaguar swerves to avoid a terrified dog which has innocently wandered into the road. The dog is unharmed. Sean"s driver is glad to have company. Someone to witness his driving skill. He squeezes past two articulated lorries and hurtles onward.

Sean is writhing inside as he confronts how difficult he finds true openness. Spontaneity. He was a mouse, not a man, when Catrin Rossini had said, "Ti amo, ti amo, Sean."

"I really like you, too," he had replied.

Afraid of the love word. Ungenerous. Pathetic. He is not sure whether she has forgiven him that. Though she has never reproached him.

"There you are, chummy. The M6!"

Sean's Spitfire pilot nods in the direction of a blue and white sign. His left hand has been clutching his chest through the last few miles.

"I'm going to drop you here, and then head back."
He jerks to a halt, momentarily letting go of his chest to engage the hand-brake.

"This alright for you?"

"Great, thanks."

"Oh, one thing before you go. My wife's threatened to leave me. On top of everything else. How could someone do that?"

Sean replies as he climbs out of the car.

"I'm very sorry to hear that. I really hope things work out for the best."

He recalls a phrase Father Columbus always used and he uses it now, "I'll be remembering you in my prayers…"

The Spitfire pilot forces out a few last words.

"I don't think I'd have picked you up if I'd known you were with the God-squad!"

His face contorts with pain or a twisted grin as he yanks the passenger door shut. Chocks away. The car moves off jerkily. Picks up speed. Is gone.

Sean is alone at the roadside. It is dark. There is very little traffic. For the first time he confronts the reality of the dilemma he faces. The dilemma which he has created through his own thoughtlessness.

He has met Bernadette, whom he had not seen since childhood, in Liverpool in the Cathedral of Christ the King.

Chapter 8

Bernadette. Not seen since childhood. Whom Sean has found again. Whom he first met when staying at his grandparents' house in Llangollen where Bernadette's parents, Mr. and Mrs. Schwackenberg, own a guest house.

Sean meets Bernadette one Wednesday, early in the term. She is with her mother in Liverpool, visiting the Catholic Cathedral Of Christ The King.

"Hey... isn't that Sean, Bernadette?"

Sean is emerging from a confessional box and is about to kneel to say his Penance. Three Hail Marys. 'Hail, Mary, full of grace, the Lord is with thee. Blessed art thou amongst women, and blessed is the fruit of thy womb, Jesus...'

Sean hears excited whispers.

"Quiet, Mum. Leave him..."

"It is... It IS him. Sean? Ya? It is!"

Sean stands up. Turns. Shakes hands.

"Mrs. Schwackenberg... Bernadette... How nice to see you and what a surprise..."

Mrs. Schwackenberg looks at Sean as if he has just risen from the dead. He cannot help noticing that Bernadette blushes. Bernadette has grown taller but he can still see the young girl he once knew. Her gaze is very direct and open and she is wearing a Fair-Isle bobble-hat, a tightly belted car coat and Hush Puppy boots.

In her turn, Mrs. Schwackenberg looks Sean up and down. His tweed jacket, blue polo neck, brown cords and his trusty brogues.

"Well, well. So many years since we saw you at the house. You must com... really, you must."

A devout woman. Sean remembers the holy water fonts beside each of the doorways in the hallway at Llangollen. Seeing Sean at Confession on a weekday, Mrs. Schwackenberg would think it good, would think Sean was turning into a very nice young man.

"So what brings you to Liverpool, Sean?"

"I'm studying law, Mrs. Schwackenberg."

"Ahh... at the university?"

"The College of Commerce. In Tithebarn Street."

"How wonder-fool..."

"Hoping to become a barrister."

"Wow, love-ly... How clever of you."

Sean pauses, thinking Mrs. Schwackenberg and Bernadette may depart, but Mrs. Schwackenberg lays her hand on his forearm and turns her body towards Bernadette.

"You won't believe this, Sean. Bernadette is coming here, too. Here in Liverpool. For the babies... the little babies..."

Bernadette's eyes are like a startled fawn's. Glittering. Their colour indefinable.

"I'll be nursing at the premature baby unit, Sean. The Liverpool Maternity Hospital."

"That's brilliant. I'm in digs just over the water, in New Brighton." Sean is remembering the Schwackenberg's garden – the carefree games. "We could meet up?" he blurts out. Making contact with somebody he knows well is an attractive idea at a time when he is mixing with so many people he has not known long.

Bernadette puts a hand on the curve of her hip. Nods briefly.

"Isn't the Cathedral beautiful, Sean?" Mrs. Schwackenberg grasps Sean's forearm again, raising her eyes to the stained glass crown above their heads.

"Yes, Mrs. Schwackenberg."

"Such beautiful colours; see how they change almost every second in the sunlight."

Mrs. Schwackenberg, enraptured, keeps staring up; then turns to Sean.

"And, you come here every day, Sean, to the Confession?"

"Not every day, Mrs. Schwackenberg, but I pop up here pretty often, when there's enough time between lectures."

"So inspiring!... " Mrs. Schwackenberg takes a last look at the beautiful stained glass, genuflects in the direction of The Holy Sacrament, dips her fingers into a Holy Water font and makes the Sign Of The Cross before bidding Sean farewell. As she and Bernadette leave they hug Sean warmly and he is transported back to his visits to their home during his and Bernadette's childhood years.

After they leave, Sean lingers in the cathedral looking afresh at the design of the roof. Built like an inverted funnel, he reflects. A rocket launcher. To propel saved souls to their heavenly reward. Some ditch in The Mersey. Or they clatter back to earth on the road beside the cathedral, Mount Pleasant, desperate, like him. They have to try again. Searching for forgiveness that lasts. Perfect peace of mind.

As he strolls around the central altar Sean cannot stop himself imagining Bernadette in her nurse's uniform - an elasticated blue belt wrapped tightly around her starched uniform, accentuating her womanly form; while she tends to the babies, feeds them through little plastic tubes and lovingly strokes their tiny heads where they lie limply in their incubators so helpless and in need of her immense kindness. Finally, in a panic, he remembers his unfinished Penance. He has to keep finding forgiveness. Somehow. He must recite three prayers, three Hail Marys. He kneels down, bows his head, says the prayers, then dashes from the Cathedral to his lecture on Roman Law. As he jogs to his lecture he examines his conscience and faces the fact that how he thought of Bernadette in her nurse's uniform was a sinful thought which he must confess the next time he goes to Confession. He thinks the priest will probably think it is only a Venial sin and not a Mortal sin because it was a sinful thought and not a sinful action.

More calmly Sean recalls how he used to be sent around to play with the Schwackenberg children during visits to his grandparents during the school holidays. Bernadette's older sister and brother organized everything. Sean and Bernadette followed. Did as they were told. Maybe they bonded then. The obedient younger ones. Playing games. Tennis. French cricket. Frog races. Golf - one putter, a ball, an enamel mug sunk into the lawn. Bernadette, Sean remembers her cascading brown curls. Quick. Sylph-like. Time slipping away inside the guest house, never-ending in the garden.

The grounds of the house were enclosed behind a high wall. Smooth red, Ruabon brick. The garden was extensive. There were pillars at the start of the driveway with stone cannon balls on top; magnolia trees, swaying poplars, towering chestnut trees and deep shadows in the laurel bushes. Sean would whistle loudly as he approached the house hoping to meet one of the children to keep him company as he walked up their intimidating driveway.

The guesthouse customers were mysterious, almost threatening, like characters in an Agatha Christie mystery. There were travelling salesmen with soap and brushes and Brylcreem and free samples of purple shoe polish, and visiting priests, strolling languidly - breviaries in hand - reading their daily office on the lawn, like jackdaws after rain. There were coal mine managers in sturdy shoes and nylon socks, and petty criminals on the run – identified only when the silver cutlery was found to be missing and their unpaid bills turned up in the litter bin.

"Their need is greater than ours, I think. Yes?" A sadly resigned Mr. Schwackenberg would shrug.

Honeymooning couples often stayed because Llangollen was on the beautiful River Dee and on the nearby canal there were romantic rides to be had in barges pulled by giant horses. Gilbert Harding had stayed once after giving a talk in nearby Wrexham. The guests came and went. The friendly ones slipped the children sixpence or a shilling but most were a breed apart moving in other worlds, resting briefly in Llangollen before moving on.

Once, on a weekend in July, there were Spanish singers and dancers performing on the lawn dressed in tight-fitting black and red outfits. They were to compete next day in the Llangollen International Eisteddfod. They postured proudly, stamped their feet, cried out. A white hot light was imported from the Spanish plains and beamed into every corner of the Schwackenberg's garden. The men, like quivering birds in a courtship dance, were close to yet not touching their seemingly-contemptuous partners. The women whirled fans with their long pale fingers, their eyes glittering like coal hewn from the darkness of the mines beneath their feet. Something cruel yet powerful was enacted. The restrained, passionate movements of the dancers left Sean speechless, hardly daring to breathe.

When the dancers retired indoors Sean and the other children were left to get on with the important business of playing what they called the Llangollen Olympics, in the cool evening breeze which by now was blowing down from the mountains. Theirs, theirs alone: the golf course, the tennis courts, the lily pond, the frogs.

Frog racing is their favourite sport. Benadette's brother lines up four frogs beside the pond and points them in the same direction.

"First frog to that twig, wins. O.K.? Go!"

They each press their frog's lower back tentatively. The frogs do not move at first thinking the children's fingers are just raindrops. They press down on the frogs' backs again. Sean's frog suddenly hops away in the direction of the pond. An escape bid. Bernadette's brother's frog heads off in the other direction and he guides it towards the twig using cupped hands. Sean loses his altogether. It climbs aboard a lily pad. The other three are off now like thick elastic bands spinning into space, rising and falling in perfect arcs. The children all hop around after them.

"Mine's winning," squeals Bernadette. Hers is nearly at the twig.

Her brother moves the twig.

Sean's frog now looks petrified. Only its throat is moving. Pulsating. Gulping back the tears it wants to shed.

"There. Mine won." Bernadette's brother announces as he places the twig next to his frog. Bernadette and her sister seem not to mind.

"Mine was called, Sean," Bernadette says to nobody in particular. He is a nice looking frog. Average size. A good hopper. But he certainly looks nothing like me, thinks Sean.

Thirst drives them indoors. Into the hallway of the house. For quartered oranges dipped into white granulated sugar. Home made ginger beer.

Sean follows the other children into the house. The hallway is dark even on the sunniest of days. The focal point is a statue, nearly as tall as Bernadette's father. It is Jesus, clad in snow-white robes, his bright red heart displayed on his chest. There is a plaque with a prayer to the Sacred Heart of Jesus and a ruby lamp which casts a ghostly red glow over all - the hallway could double as a photographer's dark room where tricks are played on the eyes, and images stay in the mind's eye even when the eye no longer sees them.

All these thoughts and images of Bernadette crowd into Sean's mind as he stands at the roadside on his journey to see Catrin in London, hoping that he will not have to wait long for another lift. He encourages himself with the words uttered by Mr. Driscoll on the ferry, 'You're alright, you. You are young. You will be alright'. He desperately hopes everything will be alright.

All the while Bernadette is sleeping soundly in her room at the nurses home near the Liverpool Maternity Hospital. She has moved there from Llangollen four weeks earlier. She loves her room, the premature baby unit, and all the other staff. She loves being independent. She loves Liverpool. She is happy.

As she sleeps, she dreams of being weightless and gliding above the clouds with the gentlest, coolest breeze imaginable caressing her face. Earlier in the day she has been to The Silver Blades Ice Rink for the first time. One of the Doctors, Dr Oliver Hahn, had taken her. The other nurses call him 'Dr Honey' because of his surname, and because they all like him. He is tall and blonde. For some reason, Dr Honey has made clear he should play a part in making Nurse Schwackenburg welcome. He tells people it is because he remembers how he felt when he first started at the hospital. He has nick-named her 'Nurse-Shining-Bright-Eyes'.

In her dream, Bernadette now speeds smoothly across a frozen lake. There is someone by her side holding her by one of her furry mittens. There is music, 'A Whiter Shade Of Pale'. Beside the lake, she notices transparent cubes covered in frost. She looks into what she realizes are dozens of frosty incubators with tiny babies inside. Removing her mittens she tends to them in their distress, feeds them through little plastic tubes, gently strokes them as they lie there limply, then watches in wonder as one by one they emerge from their frosty cubes and start skating on the ice like an army of mini Eskimos.

Chapter 9

Going to Confession at the Cathedral is a safety valve where Sean rids himself of the guilt he feels about everything. It is during the evenings at his New Brighton digs when loneliness and distractions steal up on him. He knows he will have to study hard if he is to get his law degree. He wants to study.

The two other law students in the digs, Owain and Kevin, remain in the dining room after the evening meal. It is then they commit to memory their notes from that day's lectures. They test each other to check they know their stuff managing to ignore the noisy chatter of the other guests who are hard-drinking Scottish scaffold erectors killing time after their meal, pausing before heading out to the pubs. Sean reads over his notes but the legal concepts he finds there are beyond his experience of the world. In his world there is right and wrong and, so long as you have faith in God, all will be well. The harsh truth, Sean realizes, is that none of the law lectures are easy to memorize because it feels like learning a foreign language without a dictionary.

Roman Law lectures are a good example. The Roman Law lecturer, Augustus Jones, takes up a commanding position, like a Roman Centurion, at the front of the lecture room. He has legs like tree trunks and his beard is a pencil-thin outline around his determined chin. He believes Roman Law should still be the law of the land.

"Roman Law is one of the greatest things that has happened in the world..." he barks, on the first morning.

Sean is opening his new briefcase, looking around at the other students, extracting A4 lined paper, struggling to get the top off his biro.

"Roman Law enlarges the mind... even the most feeble mind..."

"This could be really good," Sean, hurrying, murmurs to himself.

Augustus Jones tells them that much wisdom is contained within the Institutes of Justinian.

"All men are either free or slaves..."

Free or enslaved. It gets Sean thinking. Is he one, or the other? A definition of freedom?

"Mr. Jones?"

"Who speaks?"

"Me, sir."

"I, sir."

"Sorry. I, sir."

"So be it, young man. It will greatly please me if you will simply listen to me. You will find answers to any questions which may enter your minds by simply paying close attention to my lecture. May we proceed on that presumption?"

"Yes, sir."

There is a heavy silence.

Augustus Jones continues. "Freedom is a man's capacity to do what he pleases, unless prevented by force of law..."

Sean is free to do many things. He has no desire to break the law. But who decides what laws should be made? Who should interpret them? Who is entitled to enforce them? Impertinent questions. Sean sits quietly and listens.

"There is no difference in the condition of slaves. In the condition of free men, there are many differences; for they are either born free - ingenui, or made free - libertini." Augustus Jones continues with the authority of a battle-hardened campaigner.

Owain is in Sean's group and occupies a seat in the front row. He has a large frame and his chair always looks too small for him. All Sean sees of him is a bush of ginger hair which curls over the collar of his denim jacket. Sean notices Owain reacting to every part of the lecture, shaking his head, sighing, writing his notes fast and furiously.

Sean's first meeting with Owain was at their digs in New Brighton.

"Where you from?" Owain asks abruptly.

When Sean tells him he is from Cardiff, Owain grabs him by both shoulders.

"Cardiff? You for a free Wales, then? Are you? Are you?"

"I don't see why not, Owain."

From North Wales, Owain. He tells Sean things about the absence of freedom in the valley where he was brought up. How they built the Tryweryn Dam in North Wales a few years before, to provide water for Liverpool Corporation. They had flooded his father's farm and all the rest of the village so that they could pipe the water to Liverpool.

"Took our land, homes, even our bloody rain-water."

That first afternoon, Sean and Owain walk to West Kirby on the western shore of The Wirral. The tide is out.

"See those sandbanks?" Owain asks, "...Wales, across the estuary there? This land we are on is joined to Wales by the sandbanks and the River Dee. Can you see it? It should be part of Wales, shouldn't it?"

"Oh, yes. I guess it should." Standing there with Owain, affected by his certainty, Sean can see it. And he wants to make friends.

"Dyfrdwy,.." Owain says the word meaningfully.

"What?"

"That's Welsh for 'The River Dee' - 'Dyfrdwy'."

On their way back to New Brighton Sean ponders not only the theft of Wales's water but the acquisition of its land by foreign powers. He is humbled, realizing how little he knows about the country where he grew up.

Chapter 10

When they get back to New Brighton Owain leaves Sean sitting on a

bench at the seafront while he goes to buy some cigarettes. Sean looks out over

the Mersey estuary where it opens out into the sea. Brown water on the move,

mud, rock, sand; all in the grip of gravity and the passing of time. Subject only

to Nature's laws.

The sun shines weakly.

A girl in a skinny-rib jumper walks by. Sean admires her style; her

denim shorts and the red ribbons in her auburn curls. He wonders what he

looks like to her? If she looks at him at all, does she only notice that one of his

shoelaces is coming undone? Or does she see him as a young man about her

own age?

When younger, Sean had been warned that he would need to deal with

encounters with the other sex in the correct way. Puberty had not been allowed

to take him by surprise. At Sunday School Mrs. Nightingdale had explained

that their bodies would soon start to change in a big way. She had been chosen

for this role, Sean thinks, because she was the most devout Catholic in the whole parish.

"As your bodies grow there will be times when you will experience strange new feelings in various places. Your body may surprise you. For instance, you will discover hair in places where you didn't have it before. You boys will find it sprouting on your faces. Even some of you girls may develop facial hair, the very dark-haired ones anyway. This is nothing to worry about. It is quite normal. You girls can pluck out any hairs which grow on your upper lip. The boys will need to start shaving. Remember your bodies are a temple given to you by God and you must respect yours, and other people's bodies, at all times. Never touch yourselves or anybody else where you shouldn't. Doing that is very sinful; you know what I am referring to; and never forget what it says in your catechisms - God is everywhere and sees everything."

There is a shifting of bottoms on benches and a wave of nervous laughter. Sean notices Brendan has already got some brown hairs just above the corners of his mouth.

"In fact, your bodies will change shape quite rapidly. Your hips will swell, girls, as your wombs develop, and your shoulders will broaden, boys. This is quite normal and, God-willing, in later life. you will all find nice partners and decide to get married and have children of your own. There is nothing at all to worry about and, if you do feel unsure about anything, you

can always pray to Jesus for guidance or have a quiet word with Father
Columbus.

Right, children, now sing your hymn to Our Lady while I fetch Father
Columbus from the Presbytery to say a prayer with us. All together, now..."

I'll sing a hymn to Mary,

The Mother of my God,

The Virgin of all Virgins,

Of David's royal blood.

O teach me, Holy Mary,

A loving song to frame,

When wicked men blaspheme thee,

To love and bless thy name.

O noble tower of David,

Of gold and ivory,

The ark of God's own promise,

The gate of Heav'n to me...

So the girl in the skinny-rib jumper and denim shorts has strolled back.
Is looking at Sean's shoelace. It may not be the shoelace. She stops in front of

him.

"Did you know your lace is undone?"

So it is the shoelace.

"Oh, yes! Yes, thank you very much."

"Thought you'd prefer to know."

"I certainly would. Could have been quite nasty if I had tripped. Thanks a lot."

Does she see the real him now or just a tweed jacket? Sean wonders.

Could their millisecond of eye-contact have inexplicably created some sort of a connection between them? The girl disappears from view. She does not look back.

The tide slowly turns; the river mixing with the pushing sea causing the muddy waters to swirl. Smokey milt clouds drift. Disperse. This way. Swish. Nothing. That way. Swosh. A touch. Life begins. A smile. A word. A coming together. A meeting. Making something. Thinking you are in the same world. Happiness. Sean bends to tie his shoelace. When he looks up, he sees Owain hurrying back, clouds of smoke behind him and a packet of Rothmans cigarettes in his hand.

Chapter 11

"Let's talk about marriage under Roman Law..."

Augustus Jones does not dilly-dally and makes no aimless comparisons

with today's marriage laws. He is a lawyer through and through. Sean makes

copious notes. Augustus Jones needs no notes; he knows the lecture by heart.

"We begin with Manus - an ancient custom by which a wife, after

marriage, passed into the hand of her husband - in manum viri - which meant

that, legally, she was like a daughter to her husband - filiae loco. Manus could

arise from Coemptio, an imaginary sale of the woman by the head of the

family, the Pater-familias, into the hand of the man she was going to marry.

But Manus could also derive from use. If a woman remained married to her

husband for a whole year she automatically passed into the hand of her

husband, who then acquired a proprietary right over her, just as he might over

any other moveable property, by a year's unbroken possession."

Sean struggles with the new Latin words and phrases and finds it hard

to imagine how it all worked on a day-to-day basis. To have and to hold for the

man. To have and to be owned for the woman.

"Finally, Manus could be brought into existence by a religious ceremony, in the presence of ten witnesses, called Confarreatio. Confarreatio took its name from the cake of spelt, called 'far'. Spelt was a type of grain, the food of the primitive Romans. This cake of spelt was offered to Jupiter Farreus, the Jupiter of the spelt cake, during the ceremony. Hence, Con-far-reatio. And, before anyone asks... This may very well have been the precursor to the custom of consuming wedding cakes as we do at weddings today, I really don't know and don't really care. I was not around then!" Two deep vertical cracks appear on either side of the lecturer's face. His lips part. Teeth appear. Augustus Jones is smiling.

Sean wonders how many times Augustus Jones has inserted this light moment into his Roman law lecture on marriage, and how many more similiar nuggets of humour he has stored up for them in the weeks and months ahead. But he laughs loudly and joins the other students with shouts of, "That man should go far... He wants to have his cake of spelt and eat it... How did the Romans spelt far, sir, please?..."

"And now, silence."

The room falls silent.

The following morning, Augustus Jones is lecturing on Roman

marriage again. He speaks in a flat tone as if describing something unremarkable.

"Roman marriage was a relationship of considerable freedom. Marriageable age was fourteen for males. Twelve for females."

"That was really bad…" Owain's interruption cuts through Augustus Jones' flow. There are a few titters from around the lecture room.

Augustus Jones chooses to ignore Owain.
"This remained unchanged for many centuries…"

"Would you bloody believe it…" Owain is pushing his luck. Nobody has the nerve to laugh out loud.

Augustus Jones has no intention of entering a debate because he knows his next sentence will distract our thoughts from the rights and wrongs of the Romans' marriage practices.

"Of course, in this country, the old Canon law set the age at sixteen for males and fourteen for females, around the eleventh century and subsequently, the Age of Marriage Act 1929 raised the age to sixteen for both sexes."

Sean groans inwardly. Still single. Still celibate. Some of the healthiest years of his life having passed by already. He bleakly surveys the increasing volume of notes which he is supposed to be remembering. He wonders why his father thinks it is such a good idea to become a solicitor. Because he wants Sean to be set free? Respected. Not a slave. The sort of person he would have liked to be himself? A man of substance not having to opt for a safe occupation like the civil service to ensure the family's security and a modest income, as Cecil and his father before him had.

To motivate himself to study Sean tries to hang onto the idea of becoming somebody. Not really rich. Just comfortable. Owning more than one tweed jacket. Having enough to buy himself a second hand Morris 1000 to get himself around and so that he could get down to London to visit Catrin without having to hitch-hike. And on Sunday afternoons, when the buses are not running, being able to drive through the Mersey Tunnel to see Bernadette at the nurse's hostel, instead of having to walk to the ferry. As someone brought up to believe that wanting too many material things is a sin of greed, the idea of being really well off is hard for Sean to handle despite his urge to shower Catrin with gifts and beautiful things. Father Columbus had not helped, "Remember, boys, it is as hard for a rich man to enter the Kingdom of Heaven as it is for a camel to pass through the eye of a needle." Father Columbus used to repeat this New Testament quotation while disrobing after Mass, as his housekeeper, Floralba, was preparing his Sunday dinner. The smell of gravy, roast lamb and mint sauce would be wafting into the Church and Father

Columbus who had taken a priestly vow of poverty would be salivating as he spoke these wise words.

Chapter 12

It is evening. Sean is reading over his notes on Roman marriage, confarreatio and spelt cake.

His concentration falters. In their armchairs nearby, Owain and Kevin are studying hard. The Scottish steel erectors have already gone out for the evening.

Sean does not want to let anyone down. He tries hard to break free of his day-dreaming. He is aware of being the first member of his family to gain a place to study for a degree but there is already so much to learn from the first four topics - Roman Law, Constitutional Law, The Law of Contract and The English Legal System.

He envies the steel erectors enjoying their freedom in a pub or a club somewhere down in the town. As he looks listlessly around the dining room his gaze fixes on a portrait of The Laughing Cavalier hanging next to the three china ducks fixed to the wall. Sean had asked Owain what The Laughing Cavalier picture was all about and Owain had told him it was an oil painting by a man called Frans Hals.

"Not the original, obviously…" Owain had said, pretending to check for the artist's signature.

Sean had asked their landlord, Charlie, about the picture and it turned out to be an oil painting by numbers, painted by Charlie himself.

"Painted that meself - when I came out the army - in forty five."

Sean has noticed how the Cavalier's eyes follow him, like the Mona Lisa's. Clever how Charlie did it, he thinks. The instructions would have told you to apply paint to just one number, one colour at a time. Charlie had done it in his own way. It was as if the Cavalier could see everything wherever people moved in the room.

As he fails for the umpteenth time to recite his notes without resorting to looking at the pages, Sean finds himself drawn back to The Laughing Cavalier. The Cavalier's expression seems to be mocking him, daring him to live life to the full – "I can see you there, Sean. Stuck on your Roman Law. Go out and enjoy yourself, man, be like a Cavalier not a miserable Roundhead!"

Sean decides he will have a glass of beer with the Scottish steel erectors if he can find them down in the town, to cheer himself up.

He finds them at one of their usual haunts, The Golden Guinea, and he joins them at a table near the bar. They are teasing some women out on a hen night. They tell him the young one in the white trouser suit is getting married on Saturday.

"Goo' on, Sean. Dance with the lassie. While she's still a free woman."

"Leave it, guys," Sean grins.

After his second glass of beer Sean asks the girl in the white suit if she would like to dance. As they face each other on the tiny disco dance floor, the girl looks Sean up and down, like Mrs. Schwackenberg had in the Cathedral of Christ The King. She spots his brogues. Boring but safe.

"O.K."

The lights go down. The tempo drops. A slow number.

Sean blurts out, "Sorry, it's a slow one, perhaps you'd rather not?"

"Come on..." The girl shoves her handbag under her chair. Rests her head on Sean's shoulder. Fronds from her hair-sprayed beehive tickle his chin. He notices her back feels pleasantly warm through her white terylene jacket.

"So, you're getting married on Saturday?" he asks, by way of conversation.

The girl hooks her thumbs into the back of Sean's belt.

"I wish I wasn't..." She stares up at Sean as if hoping he may have the answer to her dilemma.

"Have you thought of...?"

"Yes, but it would be too hard... stopping it now? I don't think I can."

The music stops. Sean and the girl stand together, loathe to sit down with their conversation incomplete.

"Twist and Shout... next," the bored disc jockey announces.

The girl dances with frenetic, uninhibited energy; and Sean mirrors her every move.

"That was good," she says.

Her name is Paula.

"We'll have Twist and Shout again…" The disc jockey has seen how much the girl enjoyed it.

Sean redoubles his efforts. He is sweating. Words like MANUS, COEMPTIO and CON-FAR-REATIO swirl disjointedly around his brain. He wants to make Paula's quickly shrinking hours of freedom happy, before she is passed into the hand of her husband by her paterfamilias. An object of moveable property.

"Shall we go for a walk?" Paula says suddenly when the music stops.

"Sure… why not?" Sean puts his jacket on.

Paula's friends are gathering their things together. Looking po-faced. Sniffy. Sean stands back while Paula bids her friends good night. Explains she is fine. There is nothing to worry about.

Sean and Paula walk along the sand, beneath the New Brighton promenade. She wants to paddle. They paddle. She wants to hold hands. They

hold hands. The lights along the promenade recede into the far distance.

Together, they own the night space around them and it becomes easy to talk.

Paula is training to be a teacher. Her fiance is very nice, very kind. Her parents

think he is wonderful. It is just, she... She begins to cry... doesn't want to be

tied down. She hasn't seen anything of the world. Has only been as far as

Jersey. Once. The only time she has flown. She and her fiance have booked a

hotel in Llandudno for their honeymoon. She has been to Llandudno dozens of

times during her childhood. Her fiancé doesn't want them to waste money on

anything extravagant; he wants them to save up for a deposit to buy their first

home together.

Sean and Paula put their shoes back on.

"I feel guilty, saying all this... Really ungrateful."

"No, I think you should speak your mind. It is just so hard to know

what is for the best, isn't it?"

"...and why should I burden you?"

"Oh, I don't see it like that. It's been nice talking to you, even though I

know it's been about difficult things."

"I've known him since I was nine," she says. "You know what I mean,

don't you?"

"More like a friend than a lover?"

"Yeah, he's like a comfortable, familiar piece of furniture."

Finally, they walk inland towards Wallasey where Paula lives with her parents.

Paula tells Sean her fiancé's name is Kenneth. He guesses Kenneth will have been out on a stag night with his mates tonight, somewhere in Birkenhead or Liverpool, downing more pints than usual, costing him more than he can afford, thinking of his girl, showing her photograph to his friends. 'There she is. That's my girl! Lovely, isn't she?' Probably quite a tall young man, Kenneth. With bony knuckles. Longing for his wedding day to arrive; his wedding night. Willing to defend what is his. His property. By force, if necessary.

Sean and Paula reach her parents' home in Wallasey. She asks Sean to be quiet as her parents will be sleeping, before going into the kitchen to make fried egg sandwiches to share with him. Sean waits patiently in the lounge but soon he hears the sound of tentative footsteps from above and anxious whispers are echoing down the stairs… "Are you alright down there, Paula? Did you have a nice time, love?"

"Yes, yes. Of course I'm alright, Mummy. You go back to bed."

The sandwiches arrive. Thick slices of white bread, dripping with butter. Eggs, fried both sides, their yolks still runny. Brown HP sauce. Sean and Paula chatter for another hour as if they have known each other all their lives, before Sean takes his leave.

Chapter 13

The next evening, Sean cannot help thinking about Paula. She has been on his mind all day. He keeps wondering what she should do. Whether she should tell Kenneth she doesn't want to go ahead with their marriage or whether she should do what he, her parents, and all her friends expect and tie the knot in the hope that the marriage will work. Sean knows in his heart of hearts that none of this has anything to do with him but he feels worryingly responsible for Paula and her future happiness because she has chosen to confide in him over something so important.

He decides to visit the Golden Guineau later in the evening in case Paula returns there for more help. He will not be able to concentrate sufficiently to remember his latest law notes in any case and so, even earlier than usual, he shelves the notes from the day's lectures and waits impatiently with the other lodgers for Charlie to serve their evening meal.

"Alright, are y', lads...?" Charlie's eyes are shining as he bustles in with bowls of thick pea soup. He is always in a good mood by dinner time because he slips out beforehand for a quick beer at the local pub. The next course is

Lancashire hot pot served with white sliced bread, then a Lyons individual fruit pie in Carnation evaporated milk.

"Carn...ation. Delicious, isn't it? Eh, lads? Had it in the army. Tinned, see.... doesn't go off."

It is always Charlie who brings the food in. Sean and the lodgers have never seen Charlie's wife, Rose. They hear clanking pots and pans and the sound of tinkling cutlery coming from the kitchen and they sometimes hear plates smashing, or smell burning, or even sometimes hear sobbing; but they never see Rose. They know someone is there because Charlie often shouts to her to let her know how many dinners she needs to prepare.

"Eight in tonight, Rose. Right?" A muted squeal confirms Rose has heard. Charlie settles down with the Daily Mirror in the hall. Lodgers have to be in by half past six. If later than that they are not served. It's often Owain who is late.

"No dinner tonight, mate. Seven thirty's far too late. Sorry. It's Rose, see. She won't wear it. Won't wear it at all." He raises his voice, "Owain's in Rose. But not for dinner. Just for Corn Flakes, like... in the mornin'."

Owain retaliates with a pretentious and patronizing air which never fails to impress Sean.

"Man is born free, Charlie, but everywhere we see him in chains…" Owain smiles gently as he goes up to his room. From a country suffering centuries of oppression Owain has learned to bend in the wind; he keeps his powder dry. "I'm really sorry if I've inconvenienced Rose, Charlie. Corn Flakes in the morning will be fine with me…"

Sean asks Charlie if it will be convenient for him to take a bath before he goes out and Charlie agrees. The bathroom is just outside the door to the kitchen. Through the frosted glass in the bathroom door Sean watches Charlie's dark outline going to and fro carrying cups of coffee into the dining room, and hears him constantly berating Rose.

"Hurry up, Rose, can't you!"

Sean tries to relax in the steaming water. He lies back and drapes his flannel over his eyes, then hears Charlie's voice just outside.

"Sean? I hope you haven't used all the hot water…"

Sean takes his flannel from his face and places it over his groin. Charlie's face is clearly discernible, his eyes and nose pressed up against the frosted glass.

"That you, Charlie?"

"And wash the bath after, mind. Properly. With the brush... Don' forget!..."

"I won't…"

Sean hears Charlie talking to the others in the dining room.

"Don't want no grey tide marks, do we, lads? Rose can't stand them…"

Sean pulls the bath plug out, swishes the escaping water around the bath, dresses quickly and heads for the front door, but not before Charlie catches him in the hallway.

"Off for a few o' the old Black and Tans again, Sean? Is it? Eh? Eh?"

"No, Charlie. Only hoping to meet up with a new friend in the Golden Guineau…"

"That's what they all say, lad." He turns away, "Get ready for the dirty coffee cups, Rose. I'm coming through… now".

It is quiet in the Golden Guineau. Sean perches on a bar stool with a good view of the doorway into the club. Two croupiers are spinning their roulette wheels aimlessly, passing time chatting to the dealers on the Blackjack table. There are no disco lights. No music. Sean orders a pint of Guinness. He feels he should wait for a while in case Paula turns up desperately in need of a sympathetic ear. He takes several large gulps of Guinness. There is nothing else to do. He counts the froth rings on his empty glass. Five rings. He orders another pint, takes two more large gulps of Guinness, feels a familiar surge of well-being and confidence working its way around his body and calming his brain. The barmaid's name is Virginia. Likes to be called, 'Virg'. Works as a beauty consultant for Max Factor in the daytime at the John Lewis's department store in Liverpool. Her preferred tipple is Campari and soda. Sean buys Virg a Campari and soda and she starts to chat to him while he waits to see if Paula will come in. As the club fills up Virg makes sure Sean gets a refill promptly even when there is a crush of bodies pushing forward to get served. He loses count of the number of pints he has drunk.

There is no sign of Paula. Sean imagines she is having last minute fittings for her white lace wedding dress. Pins here. Tightening of seams there. Trussed up in her straightjacket. Feeling trapped. She will probably show up if she can get past her parents, he thinks, even if it gets late.

The bar closes. The club begins to empty. Sean helps Virg collecting empty glasses and wipes a few tables down for her. He notices himself swaying slightly. He straightens up to find himself facing Virg.

"Like a lift home, love?"

Virg's eyes are wide open and shining above the gleaming brass table tops.

"Oh, yes, please. That would be a great help."

On the pavement outside the club Sean drinks in the night air. He is swaying even more now the air has hit him. Virg guides him to her VW beetle.

Bright orange.

"Too many pints, Sean?"

"One over the eight I think, Virg..."

Virg is as steady as a rock.

"Were you celebrating something?"

"No, no. I was expecting to meet a friend."

Virg smiles at him like an understanding elder sister.

It is stuffy inside the beetle. The sickly scent of Max Factor products pervades the air. Virg drives to the promenade to give Sean time to sober up.

She has a portable tape player on the back seat which Virg explains is loaded with a Rachmaninov tape which is so moving it makes her feel as if she is being swept along in a foaming wave, and then becalmed. She clicks the play button. Rachmaninov resonates loudly in the Volksvagen's airtight body. Liquid notes. Immersing them in their sound. Sean begins to understand what Virg means about being swept along in a foaming wave. His head is spinning.

"What do you do to keep so fit, Sean?" Virg suddenly asks Sean.

"Swim, mainly, Virg, but at the moment I'm feeling a bit sick..."

Sean picks up a whiff of Je Reviens and it sends him over the edge.

"I love this bit…" Virg has not heard Sean's reply as the volume and urgency of the music is increasing even further.

"Ohhh..." Sean needs to be sick and gets out of the car just in time.

"You alright there, chuck? Here, let me help." Virg gets out of the car and briskly wipes the sick off Sean's mouth with her scented handkerchief.

"I need cold water," he whispers, shedding his clothes beside the car, "Just need to go for a swim to sober up. You stay here, Virg. I won't be long..."

The beach is dark and deserted. Sean hobbles across the foreshore in his briefs and, breathing deeply, enters the ice-cold sea. The water reaches his knees, loins and stomach and then he is in up to his neck. He floats on his back, lets the current take him, thinking about yesterday evening, his friend, Paula, wondering what has happened to her, then thinks about Virg. What a character. So full of life. He turns over and starts swimming breast-stroke. In the distance, he can see a street lamp sticking up like a matchstick on the seawall at the point where Virg is waiting in her car. He has drifted further out than he had intended and hurriedly heads for the shore; finally, his feet touch sand and he can stand. He makes his way up the beach. The glow from Virg's side lights is just visible in the distance. Suddenly, he sees the lights moving jerkily back and fore, as if Virg may be executing a three point turn. Then he sees red tail-lights heading off in the direction of town. As Sean reaches the spot where Virg was parked, he first sees his shoes side by side on the pavement, and then, nearby, notices his neatly folded clothes resting on a seafront bench. He gets dressed in a shelter by the boating pool. He considers

walking to Wallasey to ask Paula how she is feeling about her wedding now.

Is she alright? He still wants to know. And his swim has given him an appetite.

The thought of a few fried egg sandwiches is very appealing. But there is no

point, he realizes. It is nearly dawn and knocking on Paula's front door at this

hour might disturb her parents.

Chapter 14

Sean finds hard to bear the thought that he could have seen Catrin every day if his A Level results had got him into King's College, London. There would have been no need to hitch-hike to see her as he is now; standing on motorways in the dark, not knowing when he will get the next lift.

He has been thumbing for an hour during which nothing has stopped. Eventually, a yellow van screeches to a halt. Hertz Rental. A window on the passenger side opens and the van driver leans across, his bleary eyes attempting to focus on Sean's face.

"London?" Sean asks.

"Take you as far as Birmingham..."

Danny, the van driver, has not slept for thirty six hours.

"Lot of work on. Deliveries. Just been to Glasgow. Only one more drop to do."

Sean keeps his eye on Danny throughout the journey. When Danny's mouth drops open or his eyelids stay down for more than two seconds he quickly asks him a question.

Danny's lower jaw slackens.

"DO YOU often pick hitch-hikers up, Danny?"

"When I get tired… I do. It helps me with my driving."

Danny's eyelids start to droop.

"BIRMINGHAM... FAR now, is it? DANNY!"

"Eh? I'm not sure... No real landmarks on this motorway…"

The engine has a soporific effect on both of them. Sean feels himself

drowsing.

"CHILDREN... have you got any children, Danny?"

"Yeah, I certainly have. Two of the little boogers. Davy and D..."

"DAVY, and...?"

"Deid... Deidre."

"I'D LIKE... children."

"Little boogers they are... I love em."

Danny drops Sean where the M6 motorway ends. He explains that the

link to the M1 is not built yet so Sean will need to cross Birmingham to reach

the north end of the M1.

"Ask for the Bull Ring, if yow gets lost."

Sean walks miles through poorly lit back streets before he finally faces

the fact that he is lost.

He spots a woman under a street light in the distance. Her black leather coat is tightly wrapped around her thin form. The orange light turns her bushy brown hair into a burnished brass halo.

"How do you get to The Bull Ring from here, please?"

"My old feller takes me down there, love… when I need to go…"

Sean walks on, not wishing to cause any more confusion. She calls after him.

"You looking, love?"

"I'm fine. Really... thanks."

"Come on, it won't take long. No need to be shy."

She sounds as if she really wants to help.

Sean keeps walking, almost running, not knowing whether he is heading for the Bull Ring or retracing his steps to the M6. He glances over his shoulder. The woman is still standing under the light. Like a beautiful statue.

He walks more slowly now. Sean has been a mouse not a man for so long. He wants to be a man, whatever that is, he is not sure, but he wants heavenly music and angels singing when the time of his anointment comes, and he wants melodies to soar, arias, hymns, symphonies and romantic ballads playing in a never-ending loop for the rest of his life, when he finds the woman of his dreams.

He needs to find his way to the Bull Ring. Thumb out again. A little Fiat indicates it is stopping. It pulls in and parks neatly, waiting for him. Sean sees the driver has a smart navy-blue hat on her head. Hair pinned up. Yes, she has stopped because she saw Sean thumbing. An air hostess. Silver badge on her hat. Black hold-all on the back seat. She smiles. She looks sympathetically at Sean's anxious face. She is offering a lift out of the kindness of her heart.

"Anywhere near the Bull Ring?"

"Yes. Near there."

Sean gets into the welcoming warmth of the car. The air hostess tells him about the many places she has visited. The States. All around Europe.

"I've been to Portugal, and Biarritz…"

She shows polite interest.

"That's about it... so far." Sean ends lamely.

"I've been to Portugal too," she smiles. "I went to a place called Fatima. It's a religious shrine. Catholic..."

"I went to Fatima when I was in Portugal."

"Oh, really?"

"I went on a pilgrimage with my parents. For my A levels."

"So, you are a Roman Catholic?"

"Yes."

"Snap!"

Sean and the air hostess talk about Our Lady of Fatima. The hymn-singing. The huge crowds. The heat. Sean notices she is wearing a Miraculous Medal attached to her white leather watch strap. He remembers seeing them when he was in Fatima. He knows what it signifies. They are at home in each other's company. They know about the same things. Share the same confusing certainties.

Then the sound of the engine changes. A grating sound. The car comes to a juddering halt. They open the bonnet and look together at the engine. Neither has a clue as to what has gone wrong. They find a telephone box. The Automobile Association will be along in no time. Sean waits until the AA mechanic arrives and then has to go on. Cannot wait. London is still a long way away.

"I'm sorry, I'll have to press on."

"Do, do. I'll be fine."

They shake hands. She insists on giving him the Miraculous Medal from her watch strap as a gift.

"Take this… Our Lady of Fatima will watch over you on your journey to London."

Sean puts the medal in his pocket. He appreciates the thought. He knows that it is believed that all those who wear the medal will receive great graces. He walks on trying for more lifts, making eye contact with passing drivers and adopting a friendly stance, nonchalant, but not grovelling. It is hard to convey the right message in the dark with the drivers' headlights shining into his eyes. Most show no sign that they have seen him.

He finds a shop doorway in shadow, out of sight of the car headlights. He gets down on his knees, makes a hurried sign of the cross and prays, 'In the name of the Father and of the Son and of the Holy Ghost. Dear God, please help me to finish this journey safely so that I can see Catrin before she goes to work later this morning, and let our time together be loving and good. Please God, look after her in London and in everything she does, and also please bless Bernadette as she carries out her loving work with the premature babies in Liverpool and help our friendship to grow in a spirit of love, oh, yes, and please God, watch over and bless all my family and keep them in Your loving care always. Amen.'

Catrin and Bernadette are both sleeping peacefully in their beds, in London and Liverpool, unaware of Sean's prayer to Almighty God. The lightest draught imaginable brushes their cheeks but they do not wake.

In the shop doorway Sean gets to his feet feeling more confident that he will make it through this journey to London and that all will be well. He touches the Miraculous Medal in his pocket for luck and walks back to the

roadside to start hitching again.

Chapter 15

Sean's move to New Brighton has cut his umbilical cord. He has lost his bearings. He cannot deny it. And Catrin's move to London has affected her just as much, he reflects.

Earlier in the autumn term Catrin had telephoned Sean. She was missing him desperately and had suggested they meet up in Cardiff as soon as they could. She had driven to Cardiff from London. Sean had travelled down by coach from Birkenhead and Catrin had been at the bus station in Cardiff to greet him. Their reunion had been intense. Hearing Catrin's voice had been wonderful.

"How about dinner at ours later, Sean? My parents would love to see you again."

"Suits me!"

"By the way, I've got a new L.P. It's Rachmaninov."

"No!"

"It's absolutely amazing."

"How does it go?"

"Gentle and then it builds up, gets fast…"

"Relaxing, moving… and then as if you are being swept along in a wave?" Sean is reminded of drinking too much Guinness and being sick next to Virg's car.

"Sounds like you may know it?"

"I think I do..."

"What a coincidence. Wow! Anyway, Sean, I've been dying to see you!"

"Me, too!"

After dinner, Catrin's parents go out to visit friends. Sean and Catrin remain at the dinner table catching up with news.

Catrin has seen lots of famous people in London: Bruce Forsythe, Lawrence Olivier, and Harry Secombe, but she has still not seen the elusive Mr Huxley from the basement flat.

Sean tells Catrin about his law course; how hard it is to memorise his notes, and what his landlord, Charlie, is like. He describes crossing the River Mersey to attend lectures at the college in Liverpool, how the office workers on the ferry every morning dress all alike in bowler hats, white raincoats, pinstripe trousers and shiny black shoes, all carrying furled umbrellas. She laughs to hear how they walk around on the upper deck of the ferry, taking the morning air, some of them even managing to read the morning newspaper as they walk when it is not too windy.

Catrin plays her new Rachmaninov L.P. Sean loves its stirring quality, its light and shade, its restraint and its passion . They are transported to a place inhabited often in their imaginations but which they are now able to enjoy together, being close and loving in each other's company. They hold hands, seated on the comfortable suite in the corner of the room. Sean feels they have never been closer. This is beyond words for both of them. The feeling of love in his chest is so complete it is almost painful to endure. Yet their time apart has introduced the smallest of small changes, almost no change at all, but the familiarity which they took for granted when they were both living at their parents' homes has been tempered by the short time each has spent living away. Each of them is more aware of existing in his or her own right, yet, as the final notes of the piano concerto fade away, all Sean can think of is that he is with Catrin and she is all that matters.

The evening ends when Catrin's parents return from visiting their friends. Catrin says farewell to Sean in the bicycle shop on the ground floor. Sean takes her in his arms.

"It's tough - this being such a short visit," he whispers. "But I wouldn't have missed it for anything."

"When will I see you, Sean?"

"Later this term? Could you come to Liverpool?"

"Yes... And you come to London?"

"I'd like that."

"Vieni prima possibile... eh?"

"You, what?"

"Come to London soon, Sean... Soon!"

"I will... and we can be properly alone."

"Yes. You will love the flat... I promise."

They stand for a moment just inside the entrance to the shop. In the

light from the street lamp outside Sean can see Catrin's face. She is beautiful.

Chapter 16

Later in the term, Sean receives a letter from his childhood friend, Bernadette Schwackenberg, inviting him to Llangollen for a weekend break with her and her family. Her father had been a baker in Germany before he and her mother set up their guest house business. When Sean arrives at the house it is Mr. Schwackenberg who answers the door. His hands are covered in flour but he embraces Sean warmly, then shakes him by the hand.

"So. You are a man now, Sean?"

The evening meal is rounded off with Schwarzwalder-Torte, gooseberry pie and clotted cream, followed by dark chocolates with the coffee. Sean and Bernadette move into the drawing room in a haze of contentment. There has been a sudden October snowfall earlier in the day. Sean has brought a bottle of Mateus Rose to share with Bernadette. She suggests taking the wine outside onto the lawn, where as children they had enjoyed the Llangollen Olympics and frog racing by the pond. All is white and still apart from the occasional slither of freezing snow sliding off the pine trees and loud cracks as branches of the Silver Maple trees suddenly give under their load of icy snow.

Sean and Bernadette bury the wine in a pile of snow and leave two wine glasses above the spot where they bury it. Their breath comes in bursts in the frigid air. They decide to wait indoors while the wine chills.

Bernadette likes working in the premature baby unit in Liverpool. Likes the other nurses. The babies. The doctors. The bustling city.

They talk about their childhood; the memories they have of when Sean used to visit to play with Bernadette and her brother and sister. They talk about what they remember of each other, how, as children, they simply existed and took everything for granted. They cuddle up on Bernadette's mother's chaise longue as they leaf through Bernadette's family photographs.

Bernadette puts a record on her mother's record player.

'The Young Ones'. Cliff Richard. "...and some day, when the years have flown, then... maybe, we'll have some young ones of our own..."

Bernadette gets up briskly and changes the record, randomly chooses Herb Alpert and the Tijuana Brass. 'This Guy's In Love With You'.

Sean finds himself thinking of babies. They have been on his mind and whether or not it is moral to avoid having them.

He knows a lot of his acquaintances keep a condom in their wallet but when Mrs. Nightingdale was instructing them at Sunday school she had talked about something called 'the safe period'. She told them that all contraception is wrong because making love exists to create children and making love without the possibility that a baby will result would be making love just for pleasure which, she explained, was totally unacceptable to the Roman Catholic Church. But Mrs. Nightingdale had told them of one, natural, God-given method called 'the safe period'. Not making love when a woman is ovulating means pregnancy does not happen. She explained how to keep a chart of a woman's monthly temperature to track her fertile time and said that using self control at such times would not be contraception. Nothing artificial. It would be down to nature. Sean had also heard about coitus interruptus from an older boy but did not know anybody who had tried it. Good timing, he assumed, would be essential.

Bernadette and Sean go back into the garden. They retrieve the Mateus Rose and the wine glasses which are now encrusted with snow. Bernadette removes the cork with Mr. Schwackenberg's bone-handled corkscrew. She pours wine into each glass. She and Sean toast each other under a night sky which promises even more snow. The wine is sparkling. It tastes clean and fresh with a hint of liquorice. They hug for old time's sake and also to keep warm. It is fun experiencing the chill air on their cheeks but knowing that they can go back indoors to the fireside anytime they want. It seems natural to kiss. As their mouths meet Sean notices Bernadette has brushed her teeth since dinner. She has a fresh minty taste, with a hint of coriander.

Sean was fourteen years old when he learned the facts of life from Leslie Collings.

"Do you know the facts of life, Sean?"

"Yeah, of course I do," Sean had replied, even though he had no idea what Leslie Collings was talking about.

Sean was on the top deck of the 7A bus at the time, on his way to school, approaching his stop. There was a crush of bodies as he and his schoolmates all tried to reach the top of the stairs at the same time. Sean was one of the last. He grabbed hold of the stainless steel rail at the top of the stairs. By the time he reached the lower deck of the bus he knew the facts of life, even though he was not absolutely sure he believed them. If he had not struck lucky that day, being in the right place at the right time, Sean muses, he might have remained in the dark for ever. Jokes he had not previously understood made sense. He began to see the world in an entirely new light.

Sean and Bernadette hurry indoors. There is snow and ice outside and a fire burning within. They lock the French windows and the drawing room door from the inside. Bernadette suggests they lie side by side on the chaise longue. The shape of the cushioning is convex anchoring them together. Sean rests his hand on Bernadette's hip. He notices her suede miniskirt still feels cool from the October night air. Bernadette runs her fingers gently through Sean's hair, absent-mindedly.

"You always did have fine hair, Sean, even when you were little."

Bernadette pauses. Pours out more wine. Drinks half a glass in one go. She gazes through the French windows with a gentle expression on her face as fresh snow begins to fall in the dark outside and Sean imagines her soothing one of the little babies off to sleep at the premature baby unit where she works.

Sean's throat feels dry, despite the wine.

"I want you, Bernadette," he croaks quietly.

"That's so lovely of you but I want to keep that for when I am married, Sean."

"You're not ready?..."

"It's just the way I've been brought up. I want to keep it for my husband so that my wedding night can be special."

"That's fine, Bernadette. I can understand that."

"I want a day to remember for the rest of my life. You know, white dress, Nuptial Mass, bridesmaids... and that gift I will have kept for my husband alone... whoever he may be..."

"I'm sure most blokes appreciate that... Absolutely!"

Sean stares into his wine glass watching the bubbles break the surface, trying to pinpoint which bubble will separate next from the side of his glass and whizz its way to the surface.

"I do find you attractive, Sean. When we saw you in Liverpool Cathedral I felt the way I feel when I hear Elvis sing. Its weird, I always have a really strong physical reaction to his voice. It was the same when I saw you - and you weren't even singing like Elvis does! You were just kneeling down, saying your Penance."

"Ah... I'm flattered, Bernadette. Funny though, I remember seeing Hayley Mills, when I was really young, in a film called Pollyanna. She looked really innocent and beautiful, just the way I remember you, and I fell head over heels in love with her, although I did not think of it as love then."

It is late. They unlock the drawing room door.

"What time do you leave tomorrow, Sean? Can you stay for lunch?"

"It'll be after breakfast... I've got an essay to finish unfortunately."

"Alright. I'll make sure to give you a call in good time."

"Bernadette, I'd like to see more of you. Will that be O.K.?"

"Count me in, Sean. Life gets boring in the nurse's residence, believe it or not..."

Chapter 17

In between spells of working on his essays at his New Brighton digs

Sean spends many hours lying on his bed, thinking.

Catrin had come into his life like a lightening bolt not long after he had

learned the facts of life from Leslie Collings. They had met for the first time at

Patrick Delaney's parents' house in Llandaff. Catrin was a friend of Patrick

Delaney's cousin and she had spare tickets for a dance in Radyr Village Hall.

Getting to know Catrin had felt easy. It had just happened. She had

been open from the start telling Sean she had seen him on the bus going to

school and had liked his raincoat. It had got them off to a good start. Sean was

quite proud of the raincoat in question. He had managed to persuade his

mother to buy it after wearing a navy-blue gabardine Macintosh for years. The

coat was in a greenish check material and its belt had a thin brass buckle. Sean

wore it with the collar turned up hoping that was a fashionable look. Catrin

said the coat had a bit of continental chic about it, and she added that Sean

looked to her like someone who thought a lot. She admired that quality in people. Catrin is spontaneous in all she says and does, and Sean had always admired that quality and desperately wanted to be more outgoing himself. He could not help thinking they were very well matched from the start.

When they had arrived at the Radyr Village Hall dance, the group were already belting out the first number.

Zip-a-dee-doo-dah, zip-a-dee-ay,

My, oh, my... What a won-derful day.

Plenty of sunshine, headin' my way,

Zip-a-dee-doo-dah, zip-a-dee-ay!

Catrin was in a blue velvet dress and spent a lot of time waving at friends and introducing Sean to them.

Later, the band had played 'Michelle'. It was not something they could twist to so Sean had taken Catrin in his arms, holding her as tight as possible without squeezing. She had told him she liked the way he was holding her but he did not try to kiss her. He did not have the nerve. Not with Patrick Delaney and the others around.

That night, Sean had dreamed of Catrin. In the dream he was strong, capable of taking anything on; he felt a warmth in his chest, in his arms, his hands; as if he was still holding her. Then she was not there and he was outside Catrin's home looking in through the plate glass window of the bicycle shop.

When he woke in the morning, he telephoned Catrin and made another date right away. That had been the start.

Sean does not want to lose her. Just as she had noticed him on the bus, he had picked her out during the Corpus Christi Procession; the procession in which all the Roman Catholic schools walk through Cardiff town centre before gathering in Cooper's Field beside Cardiff Castle.

At the top end of Saint Mary Street people were watching the procession, five deep on both sides of the road. As his school passed in front of Cardiff Castle, Sean could hear St Alban's Band playing inside the castle grounds and the Saint David's Cathedral Choir singing with them. There was excitement in the air. All the people were singing loudly together in celebration of their faith.

> Faith Of Our Fathers, Living Still,
>
> In Spite Of Dungeon, Fire And Sword:
>
> Oh, How Our Hearts Beat High With Joy
>
> When'er We Hear That Glorious Word!
>
> FAITH Of Our Fathers! HOLY FAITH!
>
> We Will Be True To Thee Till Death,
>
> We Will Be True To Thee Till DEATH...

Sean had looked around at the people; all thanking God for the things they had, the people they loved, each other; for the roof over their heads, for the leather on the soles of their shoes and for having enough money for the men to blow the froth off the top of a few pints. Thanking Him for their children who were destined to keep alive their Faith in all the years to come and for future generations. The children. Adored. Spoiled. In their innocence.

He had watched a group of young girls from one of the primary schools, all wearing white dresses with a blue sash across one shoulder. Their job had involved walking backwards scattering flower petals on the grass in front of a statue of the Blessed Virgin Mary. Girls from another school had followed behind carrying wicker frameworks covered in orchids, lilies and carnations. White socks. White sandals. Flowers woven into their hair.

A service called Benediction had taken place. One of the priests had held up a circular gold-encased vessel called The Monstrance before which everybody in the congregation was expected to bow their heads. The priest had lifted The Monstrance above his head. Thousands of heads had bowed down in submissive union. Brass bells had rung out. The bands, the choir, had all fallen silent.

Sean's neck had begun to ache. He had looked up and glanced across at the pupils in the next compound. A girl's convent school. One girl had also raised her head. He had noticed her flawless skin, full brown eyes, black hair shiny as a raven's wing. She had been wearing a cream dress and a brown blazer with a blue enamel prefect's badge on the lapel. Sean was almost sure the girl had spotted his head poking up out of the crowd and that she had looked at him looking at her. During the veneration of The Monstrance. And that it had been Catrin.

Chapter 18

It seems only yesterday that he was at school being taught that priests change bread and wine into the actual body and blood of Jesus Christ during Mass, in front of everybody's eyes, using the words Jesus spoke to Saint Peter and the rest of His followers at The Last Supper, shortly before He was crucified.

"Take this and eat it, all of you - this is My Body, and this is My Blood. Do this in memory of me."

And it seems only yesterday, when he was still at school, that Sean himself was attracted to the priesthood.

Throughout his entire life, people whom Sean trusts have told him it is true. Jesus spoke Aramaic but they say the Latin and English translations are faithful to the original words. It would be extraordinary not to believe such a Truth which has been part of Sean's everyday world for as long as he has taken breath. He does not question how priests perform this notable feat. It is simply a mystery – a miracle. The power has been handed down from generation to generation from Saint Peter, who was appointed by Jesus

Himself – "Thou art Peter and upon this rock I shall build my church."

The Headmaster interrupts the chemistry lesson.

"Boys wanting to be priests when they grow up – please queue up outside my study. The Archbishop's representative is here today to find out if any of you have a vocation."

The chemistry teacher looks at the class through his protective glasses.

"Anybody?"

Sean does not like chemistry, and he knows how proud Cecil and Noreen would be to have a priest in the family. He raises his hand in the air along with five others. When Brendan Chigley sees Sean has put his hand up, he puts his hand up too. That makes seven of them.

"Off you go, boys." The chemistry teacher's Bunsen burner is already back in action heating up a red solution of some sort.

Sean and the others line up outside the Head's study. Brendan goes in first and is soon out again.

When Sean goes in, the Archbishop's representative is writing something. Maybe notes about Brendan. A pair of gold-rimmed spectacles is balanced on the end of his nose. He finishes writing, slowly puts down his pen and looks up at Sean for the first time.

"Sit, please."

Sean sits.

"And who have we here?" The Archbishop's representative smiles like someone with stomachache.

"Sean. Sean Connolly, Father."

"Sean. A grand name, to be sure. My name is Father Murphy." Father Murphy writes Sean's name down, then folds his plump hands across his stomach.

"Thank you, Father."

"So... Why are you here, Sean?"

Sean begins to think he has come to the wrong room.

"I would like to become a priest, please, Father."

"Ah, so. Sean. You think God may be calling you? Well, that's lovely news, now. Isn't it? You may have what we call a vo-cation?"

"I think so, Father."

Father Murphy looks Sean up and down slowly. As if what is coming next is the sixty-four thousand dollar question.

"And how would you say a person could know... could really KNOW, if that person had a vocation, Sean?"

Sean is not clear what the expected answer is.

"Something inside him, Father?"

The lenses in Father Murphy's glasses flash as he looks up at the ceiling.

"And what in the name of all that's Holy is that supposed to mean, Sean? He could have just eaten his dinner. That would be inside him, wouldn't it?"

Sean feels his vocation is being examined and found wanting. He desperately tries another tack.

"Father, something inside the person could be telling the person God wants the person for Himself?"

"Ah, now. May-be, young man. You could be onto something here. God could maybe tell a person He wants to use that person to help Him fulfill his Divine Plans for His Creation? And could there be other signs do you think? Tell me, Sean. Do you say your prayers every morning and every night, as regularly as you brush your teeth?"

"Yes, Father."

"And do you say them devoutly? Kneeling beside your bed?"

Sean hesitates for a moment. He remembers the copy of Life magazine he came across at home, containing a picture of two young women on a roller coaster. The speed of the ride has made one woman's skirt fly up exposing her stocking tops, suspenders, and bare flesh at the top of her legs. He was finding it hard to get this picture out of his mind when saying his night-time prayers at the time

"Usually devoutly. Yes, Father..." Sean hopes that including the word 'usually' will lessen the lie but he fears Father Murphy will have noticed his hesitation.

Father Murphy spots the cup of tea the Head's secretary had brought in for him earlier, which is going cold. He tugs it towards him. Takes a sip. Pauses. He wants to round off on a positive note.

"Sean. So, tell me, what sort of things do you enjoy doing? Do you enjoy football?"

"Rugby, Father."

"Ah, the oval ball. Excellent... Well, I can see you're a gas of a lad, Sean... And you are going to be a fine young man. Keep saying your prayers. Never forget your prayers. That's the main thing... Off you go, back to your lessons now, and pray for me."

"Yes, Father. I will."

Walking back to the chemistry class, Sean ponders on the thrill he would feel being able to change bread and wine into Jesus' flesh and blood. Yet somewhere inside him he discovers an assumption he has unconsciously made throughout his life, that one day he will find himself a human soul-mate.

Another ordinary human being like himself. He sits back at his desk with a heavy heart and a sense of dread. What if God does call him? Could he refuse? The chemistry lesson keeps being interrupted as the other boys return from seeing Father Murphy.

Later in the year, Brendan Chigley receives the call and goes away to the seminary, to train to be a Catholic priest.

Sean keeps praying as he has been told to do. He prays for himself, for his parents, for all his relatives - living and dead, for his country, for the poor, for the sick, for the oppressed, the dying and, not least, for Father Murphy. Sean knows that the call to the priesthood could come at any time, either from Father Murphy or from God himself.

Chapter 19

The idea of organizing some student events had come up one wet afternoon when Roman Law was cancelled. While riding his bicycle to college, Mr. Augustus Jones had collided with a Liverpool Corporation bus and had ended up in the local casualty department. Luckily, he only needed stitches for a scalp wound but Sean, Owain, and Kevin, finding themselves at a loose end, had sauntered across to the Walker Art Gallery.

After an hour wandering around the gallery's echoing halls, full of traditional paintings in gilded frames, they are on the point of leaving when Owain pokes his head into one of the side rooms. He beckons the others over.

"Look at that!" He points into the room.

"Peter getting out of Nick's Pool. 1966," Sean reads from a catalogue he has picked up.

The wall lights in this room are bright and on all sides there are dazzling canvases painted in brilliant, pastel colours.

"That's not art. That's a man's bare arse," Kevin sneers.

"By David Hockney. Winner of the John Moore's Liverpool Exhibition last year," Sean continues in his self-appointed role as gallery guide.

"He obviously thinks he can paint whatever he wants..." Kevin sneers even more vehemently.

"Hockney now enjoys living in sunny California..." Sean reads aloud.

"Yes. It's happening everywhere except Liverpool College of Commerce," Owain says later, squatting down beneath a large sculpture - Athlete Struggling With A Python. 1877. By Frederick, Lord Leighton.

"Why can't WE do something?" Owain continues. "There must be something we can do for the student peace movement. Must we spend our whole lives sticking to the rules just because we are law students?"

Sean and Kevin join Owain squatting on the floor and they pool their ideas. Kevin wants to make a fortune promoting dances in rented halls around Liverpool. In the end they decide they can probably get the use of the hall at the Catholic Chaplaincy for a pop concert, have a sit-in somewhere else, and maybe a poetry event in a Liverpool pub.

Chapter 20

Mr. Truman, the Constitutional Law lecturer, teaches that it is not always clear what the rules are. Behind thick horn-rimmed spectacles, Mr. Truman has the kindest eyes Sean has ever seen. He has a barrister's wig of his own grey curls which tumble over his ears, and his words are punctuated with a nervy sniff.

"Ehhh, now, ladies and gentlemen. The thing about Constitutional Law is that there is no such thing as a written Constitution in En-gland. Funny that, in't it?"

There is a hubbub as some people stand up pretending to leave the lecture.

"Now, now. Come on you lads and lasses... settle yourselves down."

There is a continuing hubbub as the comedians move back to their seats.

"That's better. Much better. Now, have you all brought your Wade and Phillips's with you?"

There is much thumping and banging as dozens of briefcases are lifted from the floor, banged down on desks, and bulky textbooks extracted.

"EH!... come on now. Let's have some law and order. Ha, ha. LAW and order..."

A sympathetic silence descends in recognition of Mr. Truman's brave attempt at humour.

"To sum it up... it's all down to the Rules Of Law, Legislation, Judicial Precedent, Custom, Conventional Rules, and Opinions of Writers of Authority. It's more flexible that way, you see? It is a messy system, hard to pin down, con-fusing really... but it's good from the point of view of them in pow-er. Puts them in the driving seat. Some other countries have written Constitutions, Bills of Rights and the like, and some would say that's more dem-o-cratic."

Owain, ever aware of his origins, asks a question about the Prince of Wales.

"Ehhh, well now... We don't act-ually cover that. Not on this part of the course. Not this year. But, as you're asking... First of all rem-ember that there's no hard and fast def-in-ition of Constitutional Law but the eldest son of a reigning monarch is in-variably created Prince of Wales. It's just a rule. He's the Duke of Cornwall by inheritance and as such is cre-ated Prince of Wales. But this only applies if the heir is a male."

"Diolch yn fawr, Mister Truman."

Owain appreciates Mr. Truman's explanation, even if he does not like it, and he follows up with a question about how title to the Crown is established.

"Ehhh, well now... That's the Act of Settle-ment, made in seventeen hund-red and one, if I rem-ember rightly. It say-s, The Crown... shall remain and continue to the said most excellent Prin-cess Soph-ia, the Electress of Hanover, grand-daughter of James the first... the he-irs of her body being Protestant."

"Was that hairs, sir?"

"He-irs, Owain. He-irs!"

Chapter 21

Sean and Owain are in the college coffee bar planning their student
action. With them are Kevin and Owain's girlfriend, Nia, who has come up
from her home in Bala.

Sean knows a priest called Father Perry. He thinks Father Perry will let
them hold their pop concert in the hall at the Catholic Chaplaincy. The others
want to hear more about this idea and Sean explains Father Perry sings with a
group called The Gracemakers which plays there every week at dances held
for Catholic students. They play pop music, some Beatles numbers, The Beach
Boys, and lots of The Batchelors. Sean is delegated to follow the idea up.

Owain introduces the idea of a sit-in. He suggests that to achieve
maximum impact it should take place inside one of the display windows in a
big Liverpool store.

"Placards outside - that sort of thing. I could tip the press off
beforehand?"

Sean remembers that Virg works for Max Factor in the John Lewis department store. Nia knows the shop well and says the window nearest The Adelphi Hotel would be the best one to occupy because it is always busy there and group members could stand on the pavement outside with collecting tins. Kevin agrees to organize placards. Sean says he will contact Virg about how to gain access to the store's window. Finally, they briefly discuss a 'Poets for Peace' gathering. They think a pub would be the best place to hold it. Kevin suggests The Swan Inn. He talks about doing readings from the established war poets but also including some modern verse and anything else they write themselves in the meantime.

And Sean remembers Catrin will be coming up to visit him sometime. He determines to invite her in the hope that she will join in.

Chapter 22

Sean makes the arrangements for the sit-in in John Lewis's without difficulty. On his way to confession at the Catholic Cathedral, he calls into John Lewis's where he finds Virg serving on the Max Factor counter. For a split-second he relives their encounter in Virg's Volkswagen Beetle; the smell of plastic seats, Rachmaninov pounding in his ears, being sick before sobering up in the River Mersey - and then watching the tail-lights of Virg's Beetle disappear in the distance before finding his clothes and getting dressed by the boating pool.

"What happened to you, Virg?"

"I just got bored, Sean. Sorry, and all that... I did wait until I was sure you hadn't drowned..."

"No hard feelings, Virg. It was my own fault."

Sean explains that he and some other students are staging a sit-in against the war in Vietnam and are looking for a suitable venue in central Liverpool.

Virg agrees without any hesitation.

"That'll be NO problem, chuck. I hate war... You'll only get away with fifteen minutes, mind, before they'll get the doorkeeper to throw you out. I'll make space in the window before you arrive, move a few things around, on the pretext of working on the Max Factor display!"

Sean can hardly believe how helpful Virg has been. He hurries back to college to tell the others.

Chapter 23

A few weeks after Sean's visit to Bernadette's home her family organize a birthday party for Bernadette to which Sean is invited. Kevin kindly lends him his two piece suit, a Burton's made-to-measure, so that he can look his best.

Sean and Bernadette meet up for a meal in Wrexham the night before the party. There is a new restaurant there. The Steak and Claret. Through its large windows they can see waiters bustling about in their short white jackets. There are candles on every table, subdued lighting, and flames flaring around the steaks being prepared alongside several of the tables. Sean has bought some Black Russian cigarettes for the occasion. The black paper is grainy and the golden tips feel smooth between his lips. He has an idea that James Bond smokes the brand, or something similar. Bernadette's hair is spectacular, in coiled ringlets, with ribbons woven throughout, matching her dress. It must have taken her hours to get them so perfect, Sean thinks. And her mini-dress is so pretty, cobalt-blue, with white daisies stitched around the hem, waist and neck-line.

As the chef cooks their steaks they can feel the flames warming their faces. Bernadette looks radiant. Sean notices himself marveling at her complexion, as unspoiled as he remembers it as a child.

Some of Bernadette's German relatives are at the party the next evening at the Schwackenberg's house. Uncle Fritz and Auntie Gertrude have a vineyard in the Nahe region. They have brought a crate of white wine. Several tall, tapering bottles stand in ice buckets. Bernadette's brother-in-law, Henry, makes a little speech to the assembled throng. He sings her praises at some length and raises a laugh when he tells how she used to peep through the door of the drawing room when he and Bernadette's sister were courting. Then, to Sean's surprise, Henry says, "...and tonight, we have Sean here. He's travelled all the way from Liverpool, especially to be here. Even borrowed his friend's suit for the occasion, I believe! All in honour of Bernadette. What dedication... Come on up here, Sean..."

Henry shoots out his arm like a conjuror making a first sweep before pulling a rabbit from a top hat. Everybody claps loudly.

Stunned, Sean walks to the front. Henry shakes his hand warmly. The room falls silent. The silence goes on and on. Everybody is staring at Sean. Expecting him to say something. Sean smiles bravely. For want of anything else to say, he resorts to repeating the same phrase several times.

"Thank you, thank you... you're very kind." It is as if he has just won an election, he thinks. When he did not even know he was a candidate.

Bernadette runs up to Sean. Tugs him away to the quiet side of the room. To her cake.

"Three tiers," she says breathlessly.

"Wow." Sean is grateful to be looking at anything other than a room full of people staring at him, expecting him to say more.

"Daddy made it."

"He did a good job, Bernadette."

"He was a master baker, before we started taking in guests..."

"I know, Bernadette… it's a really lovely cake."

A photographer from The Wrexham Leader then starts organizing things. He takes a series of photographs: Bernadette standing by the cake, Bernadette with her father standing by the cake, Bernadette with both parents standing by the cake, Bernadette with her parents and Sean standing by the cake. The cake is a masterpiece, all agree.

Bernadette has already received a lot of presents: a coffee table, cosmetics, cutlery, bed sheets, and a table lamp. Uncle Fritz and Auntie Gertrude have yet to give her their present. Uncle Fritz is struggling under the weight of a large sun umbrella with an accompanying metal base into which the umbrella is designed to fit. He lowers these to the floor with evident relief and links arms with Bernadette and Sean.

"Hey, you two. Yes. My English is not good… But good you two together. Yes... you, good. May God be wit you, alvays...."

Auntie Gertrude's English is not as good as Uncle Fritz's, yet she manages to express her feelings just as sincerely by stroking Bernadette and Sean on their backs while Uncle Fritz shows them how the sun umbrella works.

Bernadette squeals with delight. Hugs them both at once. Kicks one foot up behind her. Kisses them over and over again. Her favorite Uncle and Aunt.

"Thanks, Uncle... Aunty. I'll be able to study for my nursing exams outside now, when I'm at home. Lovely."

Sean shakes Uncle Fritz's hand and kisses Aunty Gertrude's cheek, feeling for some reason he should show gratitude too.

Things have moved fast but Sean begins to realize that some of the guests at Bernadette's party, if not all, seem under the impression that he and Bernadette are engaged to be married.

Sean lies low for the rest of the party, not wishing to upset anybody.

At last, Bernadette and Sean are able to spend some time together in the hallway. All the rooms are crowded. Guests are talking animatedly or singing loudly, "Rose-lein, Rose-lein!" There is someone playing a zither. From another room comes the sound of a mandolin.

The statue of Jesus towers over them in the hallway. Jesus's face is looking sad in the red glow from the lamp. Bernadette is happy. She has had a birthday to remember. She is nestling with him on the tiny coat-stand seat, screened from passers-by by the coats hanging there.

"Enjoy it, Bernadette?"

"It's been marvelous. Thanks for coming…"

"Thanks for asking me. Surprised me, though... when Henry called me to the front..."

"You were absolutely fine... carried it off really well."

Some of the guests pass through the hallway on their way to bed, or head off to accommodation in the surrounding area. Sean and Bernadette get to their feet to wish them all goodnight. Uncle Fritz and Auntie Gertrude are last to leave. As they back out of the front door there is much winking and waving and many knowing nods in Sean and Bernadette's direction. Sean and Bernadette nod back vigorously.

At last, the house is quiet. They wish Bernadette's parents good night and amble into the drawing room to finish off their glasses of milk as Mr. and Mrs. Schwackenberg go upstairs. They are side by side on the chaise longue. Sean puts his hand in his pocket and extracts a small satin bag containing tiny gold stud ear-rings.

"For you, Bernadette... Happy birthday... and to remind you of me."

Bernadette puts the ear-rings in straightaway. Sean gingerly passes his arm around Bernadette's waist and kisses her on the forehead.

Bernadette is wearing the same cobalt-blue dress she wore to the Steak and Claret, the previous evening. She pauses for a moment before solemnly tugging down the front and easing her breasts out of her blue-flowered bra.

"My present for you..." Bernadette looks at Sean to see if he approves. She presses his head forward and down so that his face is resting on the satin-smooth skin of her breasts, then gently with her hand beneath his chin she raises his head and eases her bra back into place.

"That was nice, Bernadette."

"Mother says I shouldn't let anybody touch them."

"Well, she's your Mum, isn't she?"

"But... it feels right with you."

"It does?"

"It does... Mother told me once that my father didn't touch her or see her undressed until their marriage night... and they've been together nearly forty years."

"That was right for them then. But I guess we all have to take our own decisions. My problem is I never know whether my decisions are the right ones until it's too late…"

Walking down the long driveway under the stars, on his way back to his grandparents' house for the night, Sean is unafraid of the shadowy laurel bushes, the towering trees, the intimidating wall. He lights his last Black Russian in the cool night air. It tastes good. As he rolls its tip between his lips he feels almost a man.

Chapter 24

Sean manages to walk the rest of the way through central Birmingham to the Bull Ring. From there, he follows signs for Coventry, thumbing as he walks.

A Securicor van stops. The driver says he is heading for the M1. Travelling to Wellingborough. He is not supposed to pick people up but he gets bored and lonely on the night shift. The driver is not wearing any protective headgear and the vehicle is slow and heavy. Sean prays that this is not the night the van is attacked. He can do without having ammonia squirted into his eyes. He really wants to look his best for Catrin.

The driver's hobby is gardening. He grows hollyhocks from seeds. He likes a bright array of colours in his garden. He has to lift the gladioli bulbs at the end of every year, before the frost gets them. Sean tells him about the cress they grew on a wet flannel when he was in the Cubs. And the hyacinth bulb he grew in General Science, on the top of a jam-jar full of water, so the class could watch its roots developing.

As they talk, Sean notices the driver looking repeatedly in his rear-view mirror. Maybe it's his training, or he does it to combat the interminable boredom he must experience. Perhaps he actually wants to be robbed, Sean thinks, for the excitement of it. He tries to think of new things about gardening to entertain the driver. Sean knows gardeners are always exchanging tips. He has heard them on Gardeners Question Time. Half a dozen different remedies to solve the same problem, with occasional agreement as to the best solution. Sean doubts that the driver is going to take up his idea for growing cress, or hyacinth bulbs and he cannot think of anything else to say. He begins to doze. He does not want to be anti-social, or ungrateful, but it is four in the morning and he has travelled a long way.

The driver wakes Sean to tell him he is ahead of schedule and will take him as far as the southern junction near Northampton. Better for London, he says. Before they part Sean shares the last of his Jameson's with him. The driver asks Sean what the inscription on the hip-flask means.

"Love conquers all..." Sean translates, sheepishly.

"Love conquers... bugger all..." the driver mis-translates. "Don't give me that! My missus upped and left last year... after twelve happy years. Didn't even bother to take the kids with her. My mother has to look after them all the time, now..."

The driver revs his armadillo on wheels preparing to drive off.

Sean climbs out, closes the door behind him and waves farewell. Despite the cab's thick steel shell there is the unmistakable sound of crashing gears, a foot stamping hard on a clutch and, as the vehicle moves off, an angry voice, "Oh, my word! Love… conquers all? What a load of lovey dovey nonsense...!"

Chapter 25

The Vietnam war casts a constant shadow over the students' daily lives but they have no time to think deeply about it, what with attending lectures, travelling to college and back, learning notes and writing essays. So they have made no preparations for the John Lewis's sit-in, apart from painting a few slogans on their placards.

Snow is falling across New Brighton on the day they go ahead with the peace demonstration. Sean had telephoned Virg a few days previously to give her notice.

"Sorry not to give you more warning, Virg. We're going for it on Saturday."

"That'll be NO problem, Sean... I'm working that day. Let me know when you get there. I'll do the rest..."

On the day, Sean calls into the Catholic Church in New Brighton beforehand, to pray for God's blessing on what they are about to do. He tells God the sit-in is for world peace, not a violent demonstration. A stunt, yes. But they want to attract attention to make a point about world peace and to get donations. He explains that all he and his friends want is for the bombing, the killing, and the maiming of children in Vietnam to stop. Also, they do not want to be sent to Vietnam by the British Government to kill people or to be killed. By the time Sean finishes his prayers he feels relieved that everything is now up to God; a weight has been lifted from his shoulders.

It is still snowing as Sean takes the ferry across to the Pier Head. The banks of the River Mersey already have a light covering. Only the river itself looks its usual brown colour.

His plan is to meet Owain, Nia and Kevin at John Lewis's store at eleven o'clock, after meeting Catrin's train at Lime Street Station at ten forty-five. He is excited that Catrin has agreed to come up from London to join them and he is hoping she will enter the shop window with him as part of the human mannequin display. Sean has been reading a lot of W. B. Yeats's poetry and has imagined himself and Catrin as a pair of perfectly matched lovers on display, transformed through their passion and love into worked gold, contrasting vividly with the grey workaday world. The previous evening he had done what he could to prepare himself, bathing and washing his hair. In a final effort to groom himself well for his meeting with Catrin he decides to have a haircut and wet shave in the barber's shop in Tithebarn Street, before heading up to Lime Street Station to meet her.

The barber's shop has a row of plush leather seats all equipped with foot pedals for height adjustment. Five male barbers. One of the barbers catches Sean's eye and motions him in the direction of his chair. As he sits down, without warning, Sean's chair descends with a bump.

"What will, sir, be having done today?"

"Hair trim and wet shave, please."

After giving him a swift trim, the barber extracts steaming towels from a stainless steel locker and wraps them around Sean's face.

"These are to soften sir's beard. Do tell me if they are too hot."

Sean can hardly speak with so many scalding towels all around his head.

"Is sir having a little flutter today?"

Sean shakes his head to left and right.

"Perhaps a French letter for the weekend?"

Again, Sean shakes his head, then changes his mind, squints through the towels and nods his head up and down.

"Just the one packet of three, sir?.. Certainly..."

The barber places the packet of Durex on the marble-topped sink, just out of Sean's reach. Sean notices the other customers glancing at them.

Eventually, the hot towels are whisked from Sean's face and his head is tipped back further, his chin pointing straight up in the air. The barber lathers

his face with an ivory-handled shaving brush, vigorously rubbing the foam in,

then lathers again before reaching for a cut-throat razor.

Sean has not shaved for two days. The barber is not deterred. First, with

practiced ease, he repeatedly scrapes the razor blade over the lower half of

Sean's face, before moving to his exposed neck. Unsurprisingly, the razor

frequently catches on Sean's skin and in the mirror he notices some patches of

red spreading around his neck. The barber chisels thoroughly all around his

chin and, where tiny pimples have been sliced off during the shaving process,

he deftly places tissue paper to staunch the flow of blood, then presses a

styptic pencil on top to stop the bleeding completely.

"A little Brut, sir?"

"What?"

The barber splashes a strong-smelling lotion on Sean's chin from a green

bottle. He is almost slapping him, but not quite.

"Just my little joke, sir. Just my little joke..."

The barber removes the cape from Sean's chest with the flourish of a

bull-fighter. Sean has survived with only a few banderilla wounds around his

cheeks. He slips the packet of condoms into his wallet. They cause his wallet

to bulge. They will soon flatten, Sean thinks, unless they are used quickly. It is ten twenty. Plenty of time to get to the station. He pays his bill, steps onto the icy pavements in Tithebarn Street and hastens to Lime Street to meet Catrin.

Catrin does not arrive on the ten forty-five train. At first, Sean loiters at the station in case he and Catrin have missed each other in the crowds but at eleven o'clock he leaves to meet Kevin and Nia outside John Lewis's. More bad news. Nia explains Owain has had to cry off with a sore throat. Kevin has brought placards. They agree Kevin will patrol outside the window with his collecting tin and the message WORLD PEACE - GIVE GENEROUSLY on his placard. Sean will carry the MAKE LOVE - NOT WAR one, and Nia the one reading VIETNAM - STOP THE KILLING NOW.

Inside the store, Sean and Nia locate Virg at the Max Factor counter easily enough. Their two placards are hidden in black plastic bags. Virg quickly leads them to one of the display windows which, true to her word, she has prepared for them. Once Sean and Nia are safely inside Virg shuts the panels which separate the window-space from the rest of the store and leaves them. The window-space is completely bare apart from a row of footlights which dazzle Sean and Nia as they stand side by side deciding on their next step. They pull their placards from the black sacks and then look to see what is happening outside.

Kevin is standing with his back towards the window holding his WORLD PEACE - GIVE GENEROUSLY placard high above his head. Sean has a fleeting impression of crowds of passing shoppers looking shocked. He and Nia are a strange sight circling each other in the cramped window space – mannequins which have suddenly come to life, waving their placards proudly. The shoppers outside take a few steps before stopping and returning to stare at them more closely. Kevin has taken to walking up and down and is attracting a lot of attention. They can see his mouth opening and closing. He is shouting slogans of some sort. A crowd is gathering around him. Sean and Nia hold their placards high, making sure the messages are facing the street outside. They are at a slight disadvantage because the people in the street cannot hear them but despite this they break into a loud rendition of "We Will Overcome" and chant "Students For Peace, Students For Peace"... over and over again. The people in the crowd are smiling, laughing, pointing; Sean and Nia wave back. They seem to be asking Kevin questions. He is chatting animatedly, shaking his collecting tin. People are actually putting money in it. They see two shilling pieces, pennies, half crowns, even a pound note.

Sean and Nia link arms and press their messages right against the window glass, VIETNAM - STOP THE KILLING NOW... MAKE LOVE - NOT WAR. Sean puts his arm around Nia's shoulders in a display of solidarity. He gives her a hug.

Just then Sean spots a face which he recognizes in the crowd. It is Mrs. Schwackenberg. She is putting a contribution in Kevin's tin. Behind Mrs Schwackenberg stands Bernadette with a tall, fair-haired young man. At that moment Bernadette and her mother recognize Sean; their expressions suggest friendly recognition and confusion, at one and the same time, on seeing Sean standing in a shop window with his arm around a beautiful young woman. Bernadette backs away like a startled fawn. Sean takes his arm from around Nia's shoulders. Out of the corner of his eye, he watches Bernadette's Fair-Isle bobble-hat move swiftly away through the crowds and wonders who could be Bernadette's tall, fair-haired friend.

Sean tries to think things through. He works out that Bernadette and her mother must have been on their way to twelve o'clock Mass in the Catholic Cathedral up Brownlow Hill. He had not thought to invite Bernadette to join in the sit-in because Catrin was going to come. Had not even mentioned it to her. He had hoped she would come to the poetry evening, or the peace concert. But now, he thinks, she has got the wrong idea. Entirely the wrong idea. Seeing him with his arm around Nia's shoulders.

Then the photographers arrive. Despite suffering from a cold, Owain has telephoned the local press to publicize their cause. The photographers take lots of pictures of Kevin with his placard and collecting tin, then they focus on the human window display. Sean and Nia are happy to pose for a minute or two then decide they should leave to avoid being ejected. The crowd on the pavement outside the window is causing an ever-greater obstruction. Although Sean and Nia have only been on display for twenty minutes they realize it will only be a matter of time before the police arrive. They leave the shop window quietly and discreetly and mingle with the crowds outside. Kevin is still parading and rattling his collecting tin. He wants to make as much money as possible for the cause. They persuade him to join them and move across to Lime Street Station to continue their fund raising there, and so that Sean can keep a lookout for Catrin.

Chapter 26

To Sean's surprise Catrin appears within minutes of his return to Lime Street Station. She and Sean had simply missed each other because her train had been early. She had gone into The Adelphi Hotel for a sandwich and by the time she got back to the station there was nobody there to meet her. She is wearing black boots and a long astrakahn coat; like Anna Karenin, Sean thinks. Immaculate. Owain is waiting for Nia in the warmth of the college library and she heads over there to see him. Kevin sets off for a room at the students' union to store their placards in readiness for the next event.

Sean and Catrin, glad to be on their own, walk down to Pier Head for the Wallasey ferry. The snow has stopped and there is a wispy mist floating above the river as the ferry pulls into the river's flow. Sean is keen to point out landmarks of interest.

"That's Cammell Laird's shipyard..."

Catrin takes Sean's face in her hands.

"Hey, chubby chops... Nice soft cheeks... It's good to see you. And you smell nice, too..."

They kiss in the cold, numbing air.

"Your chin is nice and smooth, too..."

"Aieee..." Catrin pulls away and pummels Sean's chest, "Don't make fun!" The mock argument gives each the excuse to pull the other closer.

They are approaching the landing stage on the other side of the river. Leaning on the boat's rail. Feeling each other's warmth. To Sean, their time together passes as if in slow motion; the movement of the ferry as it comes slowly alongside, the spinning of a rope through the air as it is thrown towards the landing stage to a man waiting there to secure it. Sean can see Catrin looking towards the horizon. Where the river meets the sea. The width of the river is deceptive, near its mouth. The estuary opens up. The sea, like a stilled sea-monster in the distance.

Catrin suddenly turns and looks Sean in the eye.

"Where are we going?"

"Charlie's..."

"Charlie's...?"

"Where I live... My digs..."

"O.K...."

They slip quietly into Sean's digs on Seabank Road. Luckily, Charlie is out, probably at the pub having a lunchtime quickie. Sean invites Catrin upstairs to see his room on the second floor. They go upstairs. Sean helps Catrin take off her astrakhan coat and carefully hangs it on the hook behind his bedroom door. He notices Catrin is wearing a red cashmere jumper. As they embrace Sean feels more than ever that Catrin is part of him and he part of her. They are one. They move as if each knows what the other wants. He thinks back to earlier in the day. How he would have loved her to be with him in the shop window, 'set upon a golden bough to sing to lords and ladies of Byzantium of what is past, or passing, or to come'. He is deeply moved that Catrin has travelled all the way from London by train because she wants to see him. To spend time alone with him. Sean's throat feels dry but he is determined to speak.

"Catrin...?"

"Mmm..."

"Do you remember the last time I saw you... When I came for dinner at your parents' house?"

"I do remember, Sean."

"Well, when I was leaving you and we were standing downstairs saying goodbye in your father's bicycle shop..."

"Yes?" Catrin looks deeply into Sean's eyes.

"You were standing in the orange glow from the street light outside. I looked at you then. I will never forget it. I looked at your face…" Sean is breathless, almost whispering as he speaks these words. Surprised he has managed it at all. Catrin is tenderly stroking Sean's cheeks, the tiny blood clots there from his shave at the barber's shop that morning. An expression of unconditional love on her face.

Her body stiffens as Sean says the word 'face', not because of the word itself but because she has heard a footstep on the landing outside. The door swings open.

Charlie roars.

"No visitors allowed in the guests' rooms! Arrite...?"

The door bounces back into Charlie's face. He roars again.

"You're no bloody diff'rent to anyone else here, Sean. Clear?"

"This is my girlfriend, Charlie. Catrin, Charlie. Charlie, Catrin."

"She could be the Pope's Mo'ther for all I care, mate... Downstairs! Now!"

Charlie follows closely behind Sean and Catrin as they head downstairs.

In the dining room, Jock, one of the steel erectors, is snoring loudly in an easy chair. There is a smell of whisky in the air. Sean and Catrin spend half an hour together there under the snooty gaze of The Laughing Cavalier before Catrin looks at her watch.

"I'd better be going..." She says it as if it is the last thing she wants to do.

"Must you...? Must you...?"

Catrin nods. There is only one more train which will get her back to London at a reasonable hour.

"O.K., if you really must – I'll come and see you off."

At Lime Street, Sean and Catrin hold hands.

"Thank you so much for coming," Sean says, as the train pulls out. "It's been great to see you. And looking so good..."

"Now it's your turn, Sean. London... Soon..."

The top half of Catrin's body is reaching out to him through the window of the train.

"O.K. Catrin, I promise."

"Yes... vieni prima possibile. Don't forget!"

"I won't. And you'll come back up here again, Catrin? Won't you? For the peace concert?" Sean can no longer keep up with the train as it picks up speed, curves away.

Catrin is waving. Still leaning out of the window.

Sean stands watching and waving as the train pulls away into the distance. Every last carriage. Until it is out of sight.

He determines to go to London as soon as possible, without fail. In a couple of weeks. When he has written up the notes of a few lectures he has missed and as soon as the plans for the peace concert are sorted out.

Chapter 27

That evening, when he gets back to the digs, Owain is still feeling under the weather because of his cold. He keeps sneezing and is holding a large white handkerchief with which he wipes his constantly running nose. To divert him Sean tells him the story about Charlie barging into his bedroom without any warning, when he and Catrin were there earlier in the day.

"He didn't! Not without knocking, surely?"

"He must have tiptoed up the stairs... and then he just charged in shouting at us at the top of his voice…"

"Didn't he even pretend that it was Rose who wouldn't wear it?"

"Nope…"

Owain cannot help laughing.

"Life can be cruel, boy." Tears are streaming from his eyes because of his cold and because he is laughing so much, "Bloody cruel!"

Three days later, Sean is on his way to Confession at the Cathedral when he sees Bernadette in the distance accompanied by a tall figure. A man.

They are walking up Brownlow Hill. He has not seen her since he saw her outside the shop window during the John Lewis's sit-in. As they get closer he can see that the man looks like a well-to-do farmer. He is wearing a shooting jacket and a cream shirt with a maroon bow-tie. Bernadette is talking animatedly to him as they walk, her step lively, her curls bouncing. Sean ducks into Hawke Street without Bernadette seeing him.

Chapter 28

Sean, Owain, Nia and Kevin are planning the peace concert. They sit cross-legged on the polished floor of the Walker Art Gallery.

Owain opens the meeting by thanking everybody for their efforts during the sit-in for world peace in Lewis's display window. A total of twelve pounds five shillings and eight pence has been raised which Nia is sending to Jerry Rubin in California to help fund the activities of the Vietnam Day Committee.

Kevin points out that it was due to Owain's telephone calls that several photographs were printed in the local newspapers and he hopes this will increase the attendance at the forthcoming peace concert. Everyone agrees the coverage was excellent.

Kevin praises Sean and Nia for their performance in the display window attracting the attention of so many passers-by, and for their bravery in staying in the shop for as long as they did.

The success of their first venture has encouraged them. Already, in readiness for the peace concert Kevin is thinking of putting up posters around the College of Commerce and on the walls of Notre Dame College, the women's teacher training college. All agree there will be no need for tickets; it is to be a free concert but they will use the collecting boxes to raise funds and display the placards which proved so effective at the John Lewis's sit-in.

Sean confirms he has spoken to Father Perry about the peace concert and he and The Graces are happy to play at what they are calling 'The Peace Show'. The main thing will be for people to know where and when it is taking place. It has been agreed it will take place in the Catholic Chaplaincy and Kevin undertakes to make it clear on the posters: FREE PEACE SHOW AT CATHOLIC CHAPLAINCY - THIS SATURDAY - MOUNT PLEASANT

The morning of the concert dawns brightly but there is a layer of snow on the ground and, from the look of the clouds, the promise of more snow to come later. Sean, Owain and Kevin have planned to play a game of bowls on the morning of the concert while Nia will be travelling up from her home in Bala. Kevin had found several old sets of bowls under Charlie's stairs at the digs and decided to borrow some.

The bowling green in the local park is deserted and resembles a freshly iced Christmas cake. Kevin bowls the white jack out across its pristine surface. White on white. It is almost invisible by the time it comes to rest on the far side of the green. Undaunted, Kevin picks up a battered old bowl and sets his sights on the jack. Eye, bowl, jack. His arm moves in a measured backward swing as he steps forward, knees bent, crouching; then a step or two and a forward swing. Off the bowl goes, throwing up blobs of snow on either side. It curves out wide then turns in as the bias in its side takes over. It slows, stops and topples onto its side directly alongside the jack.

"That was a fluke..." Kevin says modestly.

Owain and Sean compete vigorously, but Kevin's first shot is typical of his performance throughout. His aim is deadly. They play only a few games because their footprints on the snowy surface soon make the green unplayable. But they are calm. Ready to face the challenges to come later in the day. Ready to strike a blow for Peace and Freedom.

As they trudge back to the digs through the snow, Sean stops off at a telephone box to check with Father Perry that he and The Graces are all geared up for the show. A lovely man, Father Perry. Full of enthusiasm. Buzzing. Sean has to hold the handset away from his ear.

"It's going to be a huge success, Sean. Huge! With the help of God and The Blessed Virgin."

"Great, Father Perry."

"I've got a few grand lads playing the guitars with me and a real firebrand on the drums, I have so. His name is Ted Gulheaney. He used to be a friend of Ringo's…"

"I'll see you later then, Father. At the Catholic Chaplaincy."

"I'm telling you this, Sean. There are going to be good vibes in Liverpool tonight. Isn't that what they call them? Vibes?"

"Yes, Father."

"It'll be a gas, so it will, and all in the cause of world peace... and for the greater glory of God, Sean."

Sean is not sure whether or not Father Perry has had a drink. But he would not be surprised if he had.

At nine o'clock that evening, Owain, Nia, Kevin and Sean arrive at the Catholic Chaplaincy in the precincts of the Catholic Cathedral. Father Perry is waiting there with the rest of the musicians. He is wearing a floppy black fedora and a navy-blue boiler suit which conceals his clerical garb and partially obscures his dog collar. He and the other musicians are talking quietly together near their instruments.

As Sean introduces Father Perry to his friends, he notices that the priest is more subdued than usual. Far more subdued than earlier in the day. He had seemed really excited at the prospect of the concert. Father Perry keeps putting the flat of his hand on his forehead and after a while he does up the top buttons of his boiler suit, right up to his chin.

Sean asks him if he is alright.

"Oh, I've just got a touch of the bronchitis, that's all it is, Sean."

"Are you really sure you feel up to this, Father?"

"It's for such a good cause, Sean. I couldn't not."

Father Perry introduces Sean to the drummer, Ted Gulheaney. Sean invites them both to sample his fully charged hip-flask to help keep the cold out. Ted Gulheaney smiles and nods before and after he takes a sip from the flask. Next, Father Perry lifts his elbow. Sean watches his Adam's apple working vigorously against the collar of his boiler suit as he gulps it down.

"That's the bronchitis sorted, Thank God."

"Are you really sure you feel well enough, Father Perry?"

Father Perry takes a few more short pulls on the hip-flask. Gives a hurried thumbs up.

"He'll be watching over us all, Sean, of that I've no doubt."

Father Perry hurries off to find his guitar. Takes it out of its case. Starts to tune it. Ted Gulheaney is now busy assembling his drums. He gives the cymbal a cursory tap with his drumsticks to get them all in the mood.

There are three young women in college scarves and mini skirts sitting on chairs near the entrance to the hall. Sean guesses they are from the women's teacher training college.

Nia has brought a few boxes of candles and begins placing them in a circle around the dance area. The hall's lights have been dimmed and the candle flames form tiny pinpricks of light. Father Perry and his friends have acoustic guitars which they begin to strum loudly and enthusiastically, singing short snatches of the numbers they plan to perform when the crowd arrives.

Sean has invited Catrin up for the concert, pending his forthcoming visit to London. He walks over to Lime Street Station to meet her from the nine fifteen train. The crowds soon clear but Catrin is nowhere to be seen. He wonders if he should have gone down to London to visit her before the peace concert. He has caught up on his law notes but has found himself busy shaping poems in readiness for the poetry event, an event for which he feels particularly responsible. He waits twenty minutes, looks in at The Adelphi to see if Catrin has called in there, then rejoins the others.

"The bronchitis is getting on my chest again, Sean," Father Perry whispers to Sean, putting his hand to his head. Sean passes him his hip-flask. Father Perry takes, drinks and appears somewhat restored. He crosses himself.

Sean is struck by Father Perry's determination to see the evening

through. A good man, he thinks. A kindly man. His soft, brown eyes, like a

friendly spaniel's. Sean always goes to him for Confession. He is so

understanding. Never hurries him. Is never irritable or impatient with his

stumbling, stuttering confession. His speech is measured, never harsh. On

Sundays, at Mass, his sermons are more like stories, simple stories, not

condemnatory tirades. Stories from his own childhood in Ireland; descriptions

of scenes from the little village by the sea, on the West coast of Ireland, where

he grew up. And stories about the people there. How they lived. Lessons for

life. Sean often misses the point of the stories but is always inspired by the

warmth with which they are told. Like the story about the old man they called

The Captain, who, every year in early spring got his ladder out of his shed, his

brushes and pots of paint, and, without a word to anybody, put his ladder

against the wall of his cottage and set about painting it. He always painted it

white, brilliant white. Sean and the rest of the congregation listen hard, lulled

by the softness of Father Perry's voice. They go away feeling they have heard

something special. Something important. Valuable. Father Perry does not have

to explain.

But, despite Father Perry's valiant strumming, Kevin's collecting tins

are not filling up. Nobody else is coming in. A few drift in, gather around the musicians for a few minutes, then wander out again. Owain, Nia, Kevin and Sean walk around the hall and just outside the entrance bearing their peace placards. Owain is smoking something, which is unusual for him. Sean likens the sweetish smell of the smoke to the distinctive smell of a present in his Christmas stocking one year. It was a tube of stuff to make your own balloons. You put a blob of the goo on the end of a plastic tube and blew, to create a balloon. Any size you wanted.

Nia realises something must be done if the evening is going to be a success. She abandons her placard and piles the empty guitar cases one on top of the other in the entrance to the hall. She perches precariously on the top and spreads her arms out in a gesture of love and acceptance. She turns her body slowly in every direction as if inviting everybody, the whole world, to join her, and, over the sound of the strumming coming from inside the hall, she shouts loudly, "Come and join us... Our Peace Concert... Free entry... Free music... Free dancing... Free love... Come in… come and join us."

Taking his cue from Nia, Father Perry strolls up and stands next to Nia atop her pile of guitar cases.

"Brothers and sisters... Friends… Welcome!" He holds the palms of his hands up and outward facing, as if to demonstrate he has no stigmata. Is carrying no weapon. "We offer you - a Napalm Extravaganza. A concert for

PEACE..."

In the background, Ted Gulheaney smashes the drums and cymbal in quick succession, as if to underline Father Perry's words. Booompha... Booompha... tssssaaa... tssssaaa... ting!

Father Perry is not quite finished, "Yes! Thanks Ted. One more thing… Those who live by the sword shall perish by the sword. We need to tell the governments of this world, WAR IS THE GREATEST CRIME IN THE HISTORY OF THE HUMAN RACE!"

Sean, Owain, Nia and Kevin, and the rest of Father Perry's band, cheer loudly.

The flurry of activity attracts the attention of a few more passers-by. They filter into the hall. Sean looks up and spots Bernadette hovering on the fringes of the crowd. With the same man. Bernadette looks unimpressed. She does not wave. Perhaps she can see Sean is busy. Her friend stands erect. Uninvolved. As if he has just enjoyed a good dinner followed by an evening at the theatre and cannot understand what these funny people are up to.

Back inside the hall, Father Perry yells, "See if you recognize this one!" The mood suddenly lifts as he and the band launch into their first number.

"HOW DO YOU DO WHAT YOU DO TO ME?

I WISH I KNEW!"

In front of the small audience which has gathered Father Perry comes to life. He strides, struts, poses and leaps in the air just like Mick Jagger performing The Little Red Rooster.

"IF I KNEW WHAT YOU DO TO ME...

I'D DO IT TO YOU... OOO... SWEET JESU... OH MY LORD... OH, YE-HAY..."

His bronchitis is forgotten. Father Perry and the group belt out number after number.

It is going well. Better than Sean could have hoped. He looks across at Owain. They give each other a confident wink.

Ted Gulheaney announces the next song.

"And now a Lennon and McCartney number..."

Father Perry launches straight into the lyrics.

"LISSEN... DO... YOU... WANT... TO... KNOW... A...

SE... CRET...?

DO... YOU... PROMISE... NOT TO...

TELL...?"

Father Perry waves to the three girls in the miniskirts. They are dancing around their handbags. He motions for them to stand near the front and steps briskly forward so that he can serenade each of them in turn.

"CLOSER...

LET... ME... WHISPER... IN... YOUR...

EAR...

SAY... THE... WORDS... YOU... WANT... TO...

HEAR...

I'M... IN... LOVE... WITH...

YOU..."

The girls giggle and blush.

By eleven o'clock about twenty five people have settled themselves in the hall and Father Perry has opened up the bar and asked Kevin to look after it. Owain, Nia and Sean busy themselves with the collecting tins both inside the building and along the street outside.

Eventually, at about half past midnight, the band swings into their last song, a number by The Chiffons.

"DOO LANG, DOO LANG, DOO LANG...

DOO LANG, DOO LANG, DOO LANG...

HE'S SO FINE...

DOO LANG, DOO LANG, DOO LANG...

WISH HE WERE MINE..."

Father Perry belts it out mechanically as if in a trance. Happy to be spreading the message of Peace and Love.

"I DON'T KNOW HOW I'M GOIN' TO DO IT...

...SOONER OR LATER

I HOPE IT'S NOT LATER..."

A Morris 1000, a blue flashing light on its roof, drives up outside. The band stops playing. Kevin switches off the lights behind the bar. The police car remains parked for several minutes before two police officers stroll casually into the Chaplaincy and demand to speak to the person in charge. They look sceptical when Nia points them in the direction of Father Perry, who is packing his guitar away still wearing his fedora and boiler suit.

"Everything in order, Father?"

"Yes, we're all done now, officers... Thank you."

He indicates the twelve or so people still present with drinks on the tables in front of them.

"These good people here are all my private guests..."

The police officers mutter something about needing a special licence to stay open after hours and to play live music. Father Perry discretely invites the officers to have a whisky before they go, it being such a cold night. Neither police officer is teetotal and Father Perry soon has his guitar out of its case again. He sets to strumming some of the officers' favourite tunes. Liverpool Lou, Brown Eyed Girl, Ramona and There's Whiskey In The Jar. The officers accept one last refill for the road before departing.

Father Perry asks everyone to leave then, apart from Owain, Nia, Kevin and Sean. They want to total up what they have collected in the collecting tins. Five pounds, fifteen shillings and sixpence. Not at all bad considering the effect of the snow though not as much as they collected at the sit-in. Still, eighteen pounds, one shilling and tuppence altogether.

The next day Sean rings Catrin to ask her why she did not come to the peace concert. She is quiet. As if she has something on her mind. She takes a deep breath.

"I would have come, Sean. But... something came up..." She sounds weary, almost irritated with him.

"Oh."

"And it was so long, not seeing you much."

"Yeah, I realise. I'm sorry I didn't get down to London sooner."

"You know I wanted you... wanted you to come."

"I'll hitch down. I will... soon as possible. It's just that... I got a bit behind with arranging the poetry event for this week. How about coming up...

for the poetry?"

"Sorry, not this week, Sean."

"O.K., I'll be in touch very soon."

"O.K."

"Ciao, amore."

"Ciao, Sean."

Chapter 29

As usual, it is as she is dropping off to sleep in her flat in Hampstead that Catrin thinks of Sean. Her life in London is so very busy, even on Saturdays and Sundays.

Lying in the dark, listening to the steady rhythm of Penny's breathing as she sleeps peacefully on the other side of the room, Catrin relives the phone call she received from Sean earlier that day. She had forgotten all about Sean's peace concert that weekend and had enjoyed a trip on the river with some BBC friends on the Saturday, and a Sunday lunchtime pizza in the Italian café in Campden with Penny, before Sean had called her. She had felt guilty. She had intended to go to Liverpool but time had passed since Sean told her about the peace concert and she had been confused about the date because in her mind she had been expecting him to come to see her first.

Nothing could shake how she felt towards him but she worries she had not spoken as warmly to him on the telephone as she usually did. As she begins to slip in and out of sleep, memories of the good times they have spent together overcome her worry and she remembers a year ago, this time of year, the evening they had spent together on Bonfire Night at Llandaff Rowing Club. At first, with a crowd of friends in The Maltsters Arms and then the crowd of them walking over to enjoy the atmosphere at the rowing club. The huge bonfire. It had been a freezing night. She had felt snug in her sheepskin coat. They had walked a little way along the bank on the frosty grass. They had shared a quiet moment together. The water sliding by. In the background the hubbub of the bonfire barbecue and the muted roar of the river downstream cascading over the weir. Walking home with their friends, holding hands, they had interlaced their fingers. Catrin is warm in her bed. Now she sleeps.

Chapter 30

Sean heads for the library. If he is going to make a future for himself and Catrin he knows he will need to buckle down and make a success of his studies. Learning cases by heart will be necessary, he knows, if he is going to be able to tackle the end of term examinations. Today he will spend time brushing up on the basics of the law of contract. Offer and Acceptance.

An offer may be made to the world at large. But is a definite offer being made to a particular person, or persons, or to just anybody who happens by? Whether a contract is being entered into or not needs to be clear. Are two people stepping over the same boundary at the same time? Where does the boundary lie? Do the people know what they are doing? Is anybody deceiving anybody else?

Sean looks for answers in a case called Carlill v Carbolic Smoke Ball Company. The Carbolic Smoke Ball Company were selling some stuff that was supposed to stop people catching flu. They called their product, 'The Carbolic Smoke Ball'. In their advertisement they offered one hundred pounds to anyone who caught flu after using one of their smoke balls, so long as they had used it as instructed and for the period of time specified.

The advertisement said the company had deposited the sum of one hundred pounds with their bankers, the Alliance Bank, Regent Street, to show their 'sincerity'. Poor Mrs. Carlill used their product in the hope of avoiding catching flu but she did catch flu. She sued the company for a hundred pounds. The company refused to pay up. They said they had not really meant to offer a hundred pounds to any particular person, and, even if it had been a proper legal offer, Mrs. Carlill had not notified them of her acceptance of their offer. They said the whole thing was 'a mere puff' which was never intended to create a binding obligation with anyone. They came up with a few other irrelevant defences, such as it being a bet within the meaning of the Gaming Acts.

The Court of Appeal gave short shrift to the company's arguments. Lord Justice Bowen declared – 'It is said that the contract was made with all the world - that is, with everybody, and that you cannot contract with everybody. But, it is NOT a contract made with all the world...' Sean ensures he prints the key points in large letters. 'There is the fallacy of the argument. It is an OFFER made to all the world; and why should not an offer be made to all the world which is to ripen into a contract with anybody who comes forward and performs the condition? Although the offer is made to the world, the contract is only made with that limited portion of the public who come forward and perform the condition, on the faith of the advertisement...'

Sean tries to find ways of remembering the main principles in Carlill v Carbolic Smoke Ball Company. He imagines a king-size hoarding - advertising himself. A study in unfulfilled desire staring imploringly into the camera lens; a speech bubble coming from his mouth, 'Righto, the opportunity of a lifetime! Line up outside the College of Commerce, please, if you want to get to know me!' He would have to allow anybody who turned up and stood in a queue outside the College of Commerce to get to know him; so long as they wished to accept the offer he has made to the world at large. A frightening thought. Anybody could turn up. Or more likely, nobody. Sean sees how valuable the law can be helping people settle disputes, sparing them the inconvenience of settling things in an uncivilized fashion – so long as they can remember it.

Chapter 31

The next time Sean sees Bernadette is in the Liverpool Cathedral at

Mass. Bernadette is not with her mystery man. Mass has already started. Sean

kneels down beside her. They stand. They sit. They kneel back down again.

They voice the familiar responses together.

"The Lord be with you."

"And also with you."

And later in the Mass.

"Peace be with you."

"And also with you."

The priest gives the people a final blessing.

"Go. The Mass is ended."

Bernadette and Sean stand outside the cathedral talking, before going

their separate ways. The air is chill. The sky grey. Sean politely enquires how

Bernadette's family is keeping. In the silence which follows Bernadette's

answer, Sean stands awkwardly for a minute, looking in the direction of the

Anglican Cathedral and its Whispering Arch, then finds the courage to voice the question he really wants to ask.

"Are you wondering about the other day, Bernadette?"

Bernadette looks as if she does not understand.

"When you and your mother saw me in the window... in Lewis's... the sit-in?"

"Oh... that!"

"That."

"That was just one of your student things... wasn't it?"

"Yes, Bernadette."

"I saw you and that pretty girl, in the shop window. I remember. And the man with the placard; Make Love - Not War. Mummy and I thought you were all very brave… And didn't you do a music thing too? I saw Father Perry in his boiler suit and black hat, playing his guitar. Dr Honey and I thought he looked ever so funny."

"Oh yeah. That was a great laugh..."

Relief surges through Sean's limbs. Bernadette's mystery man is Dr Honey. There is no secret about it. Bernadette has told him all about what a good friend Dr Honey has been to her, making her feel more confident in her work on the premature baby unit. Sean keeps seeing her with him but he is just a friend. The tall, mysterious man in the maroon bow tie is Dr Honey. Thank goodness. Sean knows he has no right to feel possessive of Bernadette. He knows their friendship is all to do with feeling comfortable together because of their closeness during childhood; still he cannot help feeling happy to discover she has been spending time with Dr Honey and not somebody else.

Chapter 32

The Swan Inn in Wood Street is the setting for The Poetry Peace Event. Sean has heard people perform poetry there on Thursday evenings. No jukebox allowed. Just people performing their own poems and other poems they like and want to share.

Sean had thought it would be good if they could get a well known name to read with them and the others agreed this would be a good idea, increasing the chances of a good crowd and press coverage. He reads in the newspaper Allen Ginsberg is busy in Chicago and his hopes of getting one of the Liverpool poets to read from The Mersey Sound dwindle as the days go by. In the end he has to admit their best chance of getting in touch with them would be if they bumped into them in the street, because he does not have the first idea how to go about contacting them.

They have agreed, no placards for this one. Just an introduction by Sean to explain why they are there, followed by a collection at the end.

Sean, Owain, Nia and Kevin sit quietly enjoying a glass of beer. They work out that a chap sitting at a table on a dais in the corner records the names of the people who want to read and they ask him to add their names to the list.

He is a thin, sad-faced man called Mal, and it is Mal who is first up to the microphone. He is a man of few words.

"Evening everyone. Thanks for coming. This one's by Brian Patten. It's called The River Arse.

'The rain is teeming

    across the river

falling on the arse of

    a nude girl swimming

without even a splash

    & O it's such a pretty little arse

see how it rises now and then

    like an island

a pink island moving through the water

    something young and good

in the river that flows out of Lyons

    a nude arse and a special one at that

belonging to a swimmer floating

    in the opposite direction

to the shore.'

I hope you liked that. Now Declan has something for us."

A man in a brown leather jacket rises to his feet. He speaks very quickly.

"Er… This is called, How They Brought The Good News From Ghent To Aix.

'I sprang to the stirrup, and Joris, and he;

I galloped, Dirck galloped, we galloped all three;

'Good speed!' cried the watch, as the gate-bolts undrew;

'Speed!' echoed the wall to us galloping through;

Behind shut the postern, the lights sank to rest,

And into the midnight we galloped a-breast...'

Er, there's another bit, it goes something like, 'Nor galloped less steadily Roland a whit.' Never really understood the rest. I learned it at school. I just like the first bit... it's like riding along on a horse."

Declan receives a friendly ripple of applause.

A young woman in black jeans purposefully ascends the platform.

"I think I'm next. My name's Tessa. I hope you like Limericks...

'There was a young man from Darjeeling

Who got on a bus bound for Ealing

He saw a notice which said

Please don't spit on the floor

So he got up and spat on the ceiling...'

That's it...”

Several people throw their heads back and laugh uproariously.

Finally, it is Sean's turn. He explains that he and his friends are activists against the war in Vietnam.

“My friend, Kevin, is starting off our bit.”

Kevin delivers his poem in a curt, almost angry style.

“This is an ironic poem. It's called, Naming Of Parts...

'To-day we have naming of parts. Yesterday,

We had daily cleaning. And to-morrow morning,

We shall have what to do after firing. But to-day,

To-day we have naming of parts. Japonica

Glistens like coral in all of the neighbouring gardens,

     And to-day we have naming of parts.

This is the lower sling swivel. And this

Is the upper sling swivel, whose use you will see,

When you are given your slings. And this is the piling swivel,

Which in your case you have not got. The branches

Hold in their gardens their silent, eloquent gestures,

      Which in our case we have not got.

This is the safety-catch, which is always released

With an easy flick of the thumb. And please do not let me

See anyone using his finger. You can do it quite easy

If you have any strength in your thumb. The blossoms

Are fragile and motionless, never letting anyone see

      Any of them using their finger.

And this you can see is the bolt. The purpose of this

Is to open the breech, as you see. We can slide it

Rapidly backwards and forwards: we call this

Easing the spring. And rapidly backwards and forwards

The early bees are assaulting and fumbling the flowers:

      They call it easing the Spring.

They call it easing the Spring: it is perfectly easy

If you have any strength in your thumb: like the bolt,

And the breech, and the cocking-piece, and the point of balance,

Which in our case we have not got; and the almond-blossom

Silent in all of the gardens and the bees going backwards and forwards

For to-day we have naming of parts.'

Oh, yes, by the way. It was written by Henry Reed, a First World War poet."

The room falls silent. Whether this is from an appreciation of the folly of war engendered in the audience by Kevin's reading, or because Kevin is new and the crowd have not yet taken him to their hearts, is unclear.

Sean is momentarily distracted. He pictures Bernadette sitting on the tiny coat-stand in her parents' hallway flushed with happiness after her birthday party, and an image of Catrin follows that of Bernadette, Catrin standing downstairs in her father's bicycle shop saying goodbye to him, the light from the street-lamp outside shining down on her upturned face. He is finding himself increasingly distracted by thoughts of Bernadette and Catrin. The thoughts give him great pleasure yet, at the same time, leave him feeling troubled. With an effort of will, he brings himself back to his friends and their efforts to make the Poetry Peace Event a success.

Kevin returns to his seat. Sean, Owen and Nia clap their hands in a subdued fashion, in recognition of his passionate recital of the Naming Of Parts.

Sean addresses the room.

"As Kevin said, his poem was written by Henry Reed, a first world war poet. I thought I'd give you one of my own next but I haven't written any anti-war poems yet, so I am going to read a Wilfred Owen poem if that's O.K.? It's about soldiers in the first world war on the receiving end of a gas attack.

'Bent double, like old beggars under sacks,

Knock-kneed, coughing like hags, we cursed through sludge,

Till on the haunting flares we turned our backs,

And towards our distant rest we began to trudge.

Men marched asleep. Many had lost their boots

But limped on, blood-shod. All went lame; all blind;

Drunk with fatigue; deaf even to the hoots

Of gas-shells dropping safely behind.

Gas! GAS! Quick, boys! – An ecstacy of fumbling

Fitting the clumsy helmets just in time,

But someone still was yelling out and stumbling

And flound'ring like a man in fire or lime.—

Dim through the misty panes and thick green light,

As under a green sea, I saw him drowning.

In all my dreams before my helpless sight,

He plunges at me, guttering, choking, drowning.

If in some smothering dreams, you too could pace

Behind the wagon we flung him in,

And watch the white eyes writhing in his face,

Hi hanging face, like a devil's sick of sin;

If you could hear, at every jolt, the blood

Come gargling from the froth-corrupted lungs,

Obscene as cancer, bitter as the cud

Of vile, incurable sores on innocent tongues,--

My friend, you would not tell with such high zest

To children ardent for some desperate glory,

The old Lie: Dulce et decorum est

Pro patria mori.'

By the way, the Latin bit at the end means, It is a sweet and wonderful thing to die for your country."

Again, there is a total lack of any reaction from the audience. Sean decides against reading a second Wilfred Owen poem and turns to Owain in the hope that another change of performer might please the audience.

"I believe my friend Owain is now going to read us some verses by Siegfried Sasoon."

Owain holds his hands up, as if fending off the opportunity to read. He nips onto the platform to explain that he has left his sheets of poems at their digs in New Brighton.

"Well I'm sorry to disappoint you but it doesn't look as if Owain is going to be reading after all."

There is a discontented rustling and murmuring around the room. Mal leans across the table to Sean and whispers in his ear.

"The war poems are great but they like the funny ones best here... Usually, like."

Sean thanks Mal and gives Nia the tricky news straight away. He is aware that she has been really excited having tracked down some suitable poems by Allen Ginsberg, Sean having been unable to track him down in person, and she has been planning to read, 'Who Be Kind To', nearly four pages long, and not funny.

He looks desperately around the room and words spill from his lips without his brain having anything to do with the words that come out. He is desperate to keep the ball rolling and to get the audience on their side.

"Next up, it's going to be our friend, Nia. She's a Welsh speaker from Bala, but she's not going to be speaking in Welsh tonight, she'll be reciting something in English. At least I think so? Is that right, Nia? She's nodding. Oh, and by the way, Nia... I have been reliably informed that amusing poems are really well appreciated here, so if you know any funny ones, let's have them." He is playing for time but feels sure Nia will come up with something, "We've certainly heard some really good poems already this evening, haven't we? I particularly liked the limerick, and also the one about the girl's arse. Very, very funny. Any ideas yet, Nia?"

Nia looks completely blank for a minute. Then Sean can see she has had an idea. She leaves her folder of Ginsberg poems on the table and grabs the microphone.

"Hello, everyone. Thanks for having us. It's great to be here. I don't know many poems, hardly any, actually - but, I do remember one from my schooldays. It's quite short. Well not all that long anyway. See if anyone can guess the title when I finish...

'The Pobble who has no toes

Had once as many as we;

When they said, 'Some day you may lose them all,'

He replied, 'Fish fiddle-de-dee!'

And his Aunt Jobiska made him drink

Lavender water tinged with pink;

For she said, 'The world in general knows

There's nothing so good for a Pobble's toes!'

The Pobble who has no toes

Swam across the River Mersey;

But before he set out he wrapped his nose

In a piece of knitted jersey.

For his Aunt Jobiska said, 'No harm

Can come to his toes if his nose is warm;

And it's perfectly known that a Pobble's toes

Are safe - provided he minds his nose.'

The Pobble swam fast and well,

And when boats or ships came near him,

He tinkledy-binkledy-winkled a bell

So that all the world could hear him.

And all the Sailors and Admirals cried,

When they saw him nearing the farther side,

'He has gone to fish for his Aunt Jobiska's

Runcible Cat with crimson whiskers!'

But before he touched the shore -

The shore of the River Mersey,

A sea-green Porpoise carried away

His wrapper of knitted jersey.

And when he came to observe his feet,

Formerly garnished with toes so neat,

His face at once became forlorn

On perceiving that all his toes were gone!

And nobody ever knew,

From that dark day to the present,

Whoso had taken the Pobble's toes,

In a manner so far from pleasant.

Whether the shrimps and crayfish grey,

Or crafty mermaids stole them away,

Nobody knew; and nobody knows

How the Pobble was robbed of his twice five toes!

The Pobble who has no toes,

Was placed in a friendly Bark,

And they rowed him back and carried him up

To his Aunt Jobiska's Park,

And she made him a feast at his earnest wish,

Of eggs and buttercups fried with fish;

And she said, 'It's a fact the whole world knows,

That Pobbles are happier without their toes.'

Wow! I can't believe I remembered all that! I haven't said that poem since I
was at school! Does anyone know the title of the poem by the way?"

"A fact the whole world knows?"

"No. Anybody else?"

"The toeless Pobble?"

"So close!... It's The Pobble Who Has No Toes!"

Sean and the others go around the room with the collecting tins, reminding the people there they are campaigning to stop the war in Vietnam. There is a surprisingly generous response. They find they have collected nine pounds and six shillings exactly, when they tot it up back at the digs. A grand total of twenty seven pounds, seven shillings and tuppence ha'penny altogether. They agree to send the lot to Jerry Rubin again, for The Vietnam Day Committee, the charity for orphaned children in Vietnam.

Chapter 33

Sean has to wait a long time for a lift outside Northampton. There is not enough traffic joining the motorway.

He decides to walk up the slip-road to the hard shoulder. There are plenty of cars but they speed by. Their drivers know it is against the law to stop on the motorway itself.

Eventually, a battered black Austin A35 skids to a halt. As Sean approaches the passenger door he notices there is no tax disc displayed on the windscreen. He thinks it may be better to wait rather than risk a ride in something dodgy. It is nearly dawn, not that chilly, and the sun will soon take some of the chill away. The driver is a big man. Heavy. The sort of man you would not like to meet down a dark alley. Very tall. Only just fits behind the wheel. His chin almost touches the steering wheel. Sean takes in the driver's appearance in a split second but once eye contact has been made it is too late. He is unable to think of a way of backing out.

"Wanna lift, mate?"

"London? I'm heading for London..."

"Haven't got all day, mate. Hop in..."

It takes some time for the car's engine to get into its stride now that it is carrying two people. The driver nurses it forward like an unwilling pack animal. Once off the hard shoulder and running at a snail-like pace in the inside lane, the driver speaks again.

"My name's Jake. Yours?"

"Mine's Sean, Jake. Thanks for stopping."

Cars pass them with great regularity, despite Jake's attempts to coax every ounce of power from the groaning engine. Each time he is overtaken, Jake curses under his breath and his knuckles whiten as he squeezes the steering wheel more and more tightly.

The steering column judders frighteningly every few hundred yards. Jake has to adjust his speed each time, to find a speed at which the juddering stops.

"Steering'll need fixin'," Jake says.

He tells Sean he has been to a car auction in Birmingham. Is going to do the car up and sell it on. Knows a lot about cars. Learned from his Dad. Goes to auctions all the time.

"Luton," Jake says, as they pass a sign for Luton. "Make a lot of cars there."

Jake has been nervously studying his rear view mirror every few minutes. Once past Luton, he begins to relax, as if sailing into calmer waters after a stormy voyage. He starts to converse more. A Bermondsey boy, born and bred.

Sean asks whether Jake is a Cockney. Whether he was born within earshot of the Bow bells?

"You what?"

"Are you a Cockney?"

"Yes mate... So where you from, then?..."

"Cardiff..."

Jake raises his eyebrows, as if no comment is needed.

"Right… and what do you do with yourself?"

"I'm studying law..."

"Ow, no!"

One of the car's wheels strikes a bit of scrap metal which has fallen off the back of a lorry. At first, Sean thinks Jake is reacting to that, but he repeats himself a few minutes later.

"Ow, no! Thought you seemed a nice fella till now..."

"Don't you like lawyers, Jake?"

"Hate them, mate. The whole fucking bunch. So-liciters, ba-rristers, the bleedin' pigs, judges, ma-gistrates; the whole lot of them!"

"I'm..."

"Specially, so-liciters. They're the worst. Crooks, every one of them."

"Why's that, Jake?..."

"Plead guilty, they always say. Always the same. Plead bloody guilty. It'll be in your best interests, Jacob. My full name's Jacob. The court will take your plea into account when handing down its sentence. That way it'll be better for you. You'll be given credit for owning up... Plead guilty, they say, even when I really think I'm inn-o-cent!"

"Well, I hope I'm not going to be like that, Jake, if ever I qualify. Anyway, I might choose to do conveyancing, or something like that..."

"Yeah! Money for old rope that is, mate. Nice work if you can get it. That's what I say..."

Sean notices that the angrier Jake gets the more he expresses himself with the innocence of a baby, but beneath that appearance he senses enormous rage pent up in the body of a very powerful man. If Jake did not keep calling Sean 'mate' he would be quite worried.

"Drop me anywhere you like near here, Jake. Golders Green, Hampstead, anywhere..."

"I was thinking I'll go in on the A41, mate, instead of the A1!"

"Whatever you say, Jake. I'm grateful, wherever you decide to drop me."

The car vibrates and rattles on its way along roads unfamiliar to Sean.

"Got a little Floosie tucked away, Sean? Ave you?"

"I have, Jake. Her name's Catrin. Works in London."

The way Jake says 'floosie' is sensual. Sean thinks of Catrin. How wonderful it is to have someone soft, warm and wanting you, waiting at the end of your journey. In a place where you can curl up together. Her place. In her room. The warm nest of her bed. Together, at last.

"This do you? Here?"

"This'll be grand."

"Next time I needs a brief, I'll ring you..."

"Righto, Jake, thanks... But I do have to qualify first."

"No... don't worry, you'll qualify, mate. You're half way there already. I can tell."

Jake drives on into central London. Sean finds a bench on the edge of Hampstead Heath. There is a faltering light in the morning sky. Six thirty. Still too early to call on Catrin.

Sean feels for his hip-flask then remembers that he shared the last of its contents with the Securicor driver south of Northampton. He tugs the flask out of his pocket anyway, unscrews the cap, sniffs the rich, dry-sweet aroma. John Jameson & Son. He dozes. He wakes, shivering. It is six forty-five. Still too early.

He finds a small café down the road. Sean is so tired he can hardly tell whether he is awake or dreaming. He breakfasts on croissants and cappuccino, an early morning communion. Bread in the form of the Islamic crescent.

Coffee named after the Capuchin monks or maybe capuchin monkeys. The monks in their brown habits and hoods. The monkeys with their bright little eyes and winning ways. Sean wonders what on earth either of them have in common with coffee? Maybe the froth on top of the coffee is like a hood? Catrin would know. 'Vieni prima possibile', she had said to him. Sean rejoices. At last. He has arrived. Light-headed. Longing for Catrin. Longing to see her.

He knows it is important to be honest and is still confused about seeing two girls. He regards them both as friends. He loves them both as people. He wants them both but he knows he cannot have both. That would be blatant greed. There has just not been time to work everything out. Perhaps, he reflects, he has not wanted to work things out? He has let things drift because it suited him. Sitting at the cafe table he closes his eyes and silently recites a short prayer of contrition, in case he has offended God and wronged the girls through anything he has done.

'Oh My God! I am most heartily sorry for all my sins and I detest them above all things, because they deserve Thy dreadful punishments, but most of all because they offend Thine infinite Goodness, and I firmly resolve, with the help of Thy grace, never to offend Thee again and carefully to avoid the occasions of sin.'

He tries to persuade himself that no wrong has been done. No love has been consummated. There has been such closeness, real connection, sincere love. Circumstances have conspired to frustrate any final decisions by Sean, or the girls, about anything.

"Would you like more?" The waitress has noticed Sean's cup is empty.

"Please, cappuccino."

Now that he has reached London, Sean knows where he wants the tide to take him and Catrin. To a place where there is skin on skin. Her whole body against his, both where the sun tanned her in Ostia last summer and where it did not, and he wants to see her hair falling across her face as she abandons herself to the power of their embrace. Then, gentleness. Time stilled.

Sean chastises himself for indulging in presumptuous fantasy. It takes two to tango. But he believes that Catrin and he are ready to commit to each other. She has said so. Something makes her trust him enough to want to share herself with him and he trusts her in the same way.

As he leaves the cafe, Sean notices that a giant red sun has risen majestically through the chill Hampstead dawn. It shimmers with energy. Irrepressible. Close. The earth reaching its perihelion. Like Sean. Nearing Catrin again. He feels alive, despite his lack of sleep. Fresh morning air in his lungs. The sun rising just as it did on the first day of its creation, as it has countless times since, giving out light and life and he is here to witness it, this day, today, visiting someone he loves in whose company he will be able to watch the sun go down.

Chapter 34

Sean makes his way to Catrin's flat using directions she has given him. He finds the Royal Free Hospital and passes by Belsize Park tube station. Then he is on Haverstock Hill.

Catrin opens the front door on Sean's second ringing of the bell. She looks amazed, then exclaims, "Hey... Sean. What time of the morning do you call this?" She gives him a hug. "So, you've made it to London... at last."

"... promised I'd come, didn't I?"

"You did. It's marvelous to see you again. We've just finished eating breakfast. Come and say hello to everyone."

It is Sean's turn to be surprised. As well as Catrin's flatmate, Penny, a man is sitting at the breakfast table flicking through a newspaper.

Catrin introduces Sean as a friend from Cardiff; then introduces the man to Sean, "And this is Rupert, Sean..."

"My dear boy, how nice..."

Rupert stretches his arm out, energetically. Rupert looks to Sean as if he feels very much at home in the flat.

"How do you do, Rupert."

Sean takes Rupert's outstretched hand in his. He decides he is worrying about nothing. Over-reacting. Like he did when he saw Bernadette with Dr Honey and jumped to the wrong conclusion. He knows it is unfair of him to think that Rupert could be linked to Catrin rather than her flat-mate, Penny.

Catrin explains they are all rushing out to work. Sean can use the flat. Have a bath. Have a nap, if he likes. Catrin and Rupert will be meeting up for a pub lunch at around twelve thirty near Bush House where Catrin works and, as it happens, Rupert works too. Catrin suggests Sean might like to join them for lunch?

At twelve thirty, Sean opts for a Ploughman's; Rupert and Catrin choose Chicken In The Basket, a favourite of theirs. Rupert has ordered glasses of Frascati for himself and Catrin and, on learning Sean prefers beer, orders him a pint of Watney's Draught Red Barrel. Rupert insists on paying for everything as Sean's arrival in London has made this a special occasion.

"Have you ever heard Rupert announcing on the radio, Sean?" Catrin asks, "He's a BBC radio announcer on the World Service."

"No, never." Sean is surprised how Catrin seems oblivious to the possibility that he may be wondering about what her relationship with Rupert might be. He appreciates he has arrived out of the blue and she is doing her best to be nice and friendly to them both but feels she should have put him out of his misery by now.

"Do your party piece for Sean, Rupert," Catrin smiles and touches Rupert lightly on his arm.

"Catrin! - nobody wants to hear me do that in here!"

"Oh, go on Rupert. I'm sure Sean would love to hear you, wouldn't you Sean?"

Sean nods in mute agreement.

"Oh, well, if I must... 'A very good evening and welcome to all our listeners. This is the BBC World Service, coming to you from Bush House in London.' How was that?"

"Wonderful, Rupert."

"Very good." Sean agrees, reluctantly.

Sean notices Rupert has an exceptionally deep, fruity voice which could only be described as like dark chocolate.

They are all smiling after Rupert's performance.

"That's it - that's how he starts off at the beginning of the programme." Catrin looks relieved that they all seem to be getting on so well together.

When they have eaten and drunk their fill they all stare uneasily at their empty plates, fiddle with their crumpled serviettes. At last, it is Rupert who breaks the silence.

"Still time for a bit of a puff on the old pipe, I think." He reaches into his jacket pocket for his briar pipe and pipe tool. He packs the bowl with Saint Bruno tobacco, rough cut and ready rubbed. In the manner of a man for whom all is well with the world, he pushes down slowly and deliberately on the tobacco in the bowl using the silver tamper on his pipe tool. Noticing Sean watching him, Rupert explains what the other devices are for; a silver blade to scrape the bowl of the briar when the carbon deposit gets too thick, and a silver prong which he uses to aerate the tobacco if it gets too tightly packed and the smoke is not flowing easily down the stem.

"...It's this one, Sean, the tamping one, which I tend to use most frequently."

Sean notices how Rupert presses his shoulder hard against Catrin's as he leans sideways to extract a box of matches from his opposite jacket pocket. She watches him intently as he strikes a match and puffs hard on the pipe's stem. The tobacco in the pipe's bowl flares brightly and he presses down gently with the tamper to ensure the top layer of tobacco is firm and burns evenly .

Clouds of smoke swirl around them. Catrin inhales it, contentedly.

"Doesn't it smell absolutely gorgeous? I love Saint Bruno."

Despite feeling slightly sick, Sean tugs a packet of Rothman's King Size Cigarettes from the pocket of his jacket, leaning intimately against Catrin's other shoulder as he gets them out. He asks Rupert for a light. As Rupert extends the lighted match towards him, Sean notices Rupert's hand is as steady as a rock. But they are soft hands with well-manicured nails. Have probably not done a hard day's work in their life, he thinks. Yet neither have his, Sean realises, and Catrin probably cares not a jot whether or not a man has callouses on his hands in any event.

Sean is increasingly aware of being in competition with this man, this Rupert, who is merely one of Catrin's and Penny's friends and happens to work in the BBC where Catrin herself works, and who happens to breakfast with Catrin and Penny from time to time. A man who has been kind enough to treat Sean to lunch because he is Catrin's friend.

Sean draws on his cigarette, ostentatiously inhaling large quantities of smoke, and blows huge smoke-rings which quiver in the air above them, to demonstrate his own smoking prowess.

"Sean is reading law," Catrin says brightly.

"Aha! Summum ius summa inuria - I always say, Sean! What think you?"

"Summum what?"

"The more law, the less justice..."

"I'd certainly like there to be less law... Less to learn, then!"

Catrin laughs loudly at Sean's attempt at humour, and Rupert nods approvingly.

Sean has to admit that Rupert is pleasant company. Urbane. Courteous.

"Another pint of Watney's Draught Red Barrel, Sean... for the road?"

"If you and Catrin are having another one, Rupert... Thanks."

Sean has begun to refer to Catrin and Rupert as if they are in a relationship, without either of them having said anything.

Catrin and Rupert decide to have another glass of Frascati to keep Sean company for a little while longer.

While Rupert is standing confidently at the bar waiting to be served Sean notices Rupert is greying at the temples and this makes him look very distinguished, like a young Harold Macmillan.

Even with Rupert ten yards away Sean cannot bring himself to ask Catrin whether or not Rupert and she are in a relationship. He finds himself going along with conversations about trivial, day-to-day things. Catrin's parents are buying a small yacht. He asks her where they are going to moor it. They plan to rent a mooring in Tenby, the following summer. In truth, Sean is terrified to ask her the question he wants to ask.

Rupert returns with the fresh drinks. He sits down beside them, sliding his arm proprietorially along the back of Catrin's seat.

In his heart of hearts, Sean knows what they all know, that things have changed. The world has moved on. Somebody has been left behind. In Liverpool. In a time-warp; living in a fool's paradise; thinking the world revolved around him; not realizing that nothing stands still and not fully appreciating the importance of other people's feelings. Catrin. In London. Catrin has moved on.

He numbly reflects that Catrin and Rupert must have discovered they enjoyed each other's company in the canteen at Bush House. They would have been easily attracted to each other. How could Rupert not enjoy Catrin's company? And she, with nothing to do during the long evenings after work would have been flattered. A handsome, charming suitor. Attentive. Money to spend. Intelligent conversation to be had.

Sean cannot help feeling sorry for himself. It is not fair, he thinks. Rupert probably has a wife. Or, at least, has left a wife. It is true his wife may have tired of his fruity tones and his aromatic pipe smoke. His endless cheerfulness. She may well have been first to find someone new. It could well have been that, he reasons. Thinking of it like that makes him feel less hard done by. But it does not change what has happened.

Rupert suddenly springs to his feet.

"Aah, well. Back to the grind. Got some paper work to do. Have to love and leave you..."

"See you later," says Catrin quickly, "I'll just wait here with Sean for a minute."

Catrin sits quietly while Rupert leaves. Sean waits. Catrin takes his hand, interlaces her fingers firmly in his.

"Come with me," she half-whispers.

Catrin leads Sean out of the pub, a look of quiet determination on her face, through the lunchtime crowds thronging the streets and up the steps of a medium-sized hotel, just off Shaftesbury Avenue. She finds them a table and they both order coffee. Catrin speaks for the first time since leaving the pub.

"Hey, Sean, I need to talk to you."

"O.K."

"I'll never forget us you know...?"

"Forget us?"

"...Yes. You see, Rupert and me. Well, we are together now, Sean. I'm afraid that is the way it is... It's happened. It wasn't planned. I'm sorry... you and I are going to have to finish."

"I see, Catrin... Well, what can I say?"

"I'll never forget us, you know." Catrin says again.

Before they part, Catrin tells Sean where he can catch the tube. To get to the best place for hitching back.

"And, Sean, we MUST meet up again, in Cardiff, sometime..."

"Yes, Catrin, that would be really good..."

"For a coffee in town, or something like that..."

Sean hugs Catrin. Catrin gives Sean a quick peck on the cheek and squeezes his hand.

Sean heads for the tube.

Chapter 35

Sean is upset and angry travelling down the escalator at the tube station. He is not angry with Catrin. He is angry with himself; his inability to get things right, however hard he tries, however hard he prays.

Waiting on the platform he wants to be a Welsh yobbo singing rugby songs. It is not his normal demeanor but feelings are bubbling up inside him which he cannot express. When the train comes in he finds a seat and then he starts to sing. He wants to shock people. He sings in a loud voice. The two pints of Watneys Draught Red Barrel give him just enough courage to carry on.

"IF I WERE THE MARRYING KIND

I THANK THE LORD I'M NOT, SIR

THE KIND OF GIRL THAT I WOULD MARRY

WOULD BE A FULL-BACK'S DAUGHTER...

SHE'D FIND TOUCH

I'D FIND TOUCH

WE'D BOTH FIND TOUCH... TOGETHER

OH, WHAT FUN, IN THE MIDDLE OF THE NIGHT

FINDING TOUCH... TOGETHER."

The louder Sean sings, the less attention people pay. They look away. But Sean knows they can hear him.

He tries one or two more songs even more loudly. He notices some passengers look at him indirectly, at his reflection in the window nearest them. Others mouth the words of the song along with him - to show him they know the words - and he is not shocking them.

He finds himself singing more quietly, and swaying to the train's rhythm. Some of the passengers are smiling openly now. He goes through his repertoire of silly songs. Nobody is bothered. He drifts into talking sense to himself. Life goes on. Plenty of fish in the sea. Other fruit for the picking. Oranges and apples and pears and figs. Forget it. Forget Catrin if you can. Move on. You are a young man. You live to love another day. Forget Rupert. Fucking Rupert. Probably a very nice man. When you get to know him. Like Catrin does! Grey-haired old dodderer! No, no. If you do prick him, does he not bleed? Is he not human? Who knows? But Catrin loves him. Dotes on him! Even likes his pipe smoke! And Sean does not want Catrin to be unhappy. Why should he? She has always been fantastic with him but has had to make her own way. All on her own in London. When she wanted him there with her. And he would have been with her, Sean thinks, if Our Lady of Fatima had not let him down! No wonder he has lost her.

He concedes to himself their relationship, at best, has been based on some very special moments, potent mutual attraction, haunting music, romance...

'Since you went away, the days grow long -

But I miss you most of all, my darling -

When autumn leaves start to fall...'

That was it. That was all. That was everything and nothing. No contract. No Carlill versus the Carbolic Smoke Ball Company, offers or acceptances. No marriage. No passing 'in manu viri', into the hand of a husband. No slaves. No servants. No binding commitment. Just the commitment of two young people to each other. The purest contract of all.

Catrin is young. Free to live as she wishes and to make her own decisions. Her own choices. Sean tells himself he has to accept this. She has chosen Rupert. RUPERT... RUPERT...! But, he consoles himself, she has said she will never forget them, herself and Sean. They will meet up again in Cardiff sometime, even if it will just be for coffee.

Chapter 36

Hitch-hiking back to Liverpool passes in a blur. Thumb out. A Car. Thumb out again. A Lorry. Next an ice cream van. A car. Another car. Thumb out. A GPO van - back along the East Lancs Road to Liverpool.

Onto the ferry at Pier Head. Sean takes refuge in one of the ferry's saloons. The effect of the beers at lunchtime has worn off and he has a headache. Through the window he notices Driscoll, the man he met when looking for the East Lancs Road the previous evening. Sean hopes Driscoll does not notice him. He does not want to talk feeling as he does. Driscoll is pacing around the deck of the ferry dressed only in shirt sleeves. He soon spots Sean in the saloon and edges in sideways.

"Alright? Alright are you, son?"

"Fine, thanks, Mister Driscoll..."

Driscoll looks furtively over his shoulder hearing Sean confidently mentioning his surname.

"How do you know me name, son?"

"From you... Last night..."

"Is that so...? That's alright then..."

Driscoll suddenly finds the courage to confide in Sean. He is shivering. He grasps Sean by the arm, like a long lost friend. He tells him that his wife is in hospital.

"Not much hope, y'see..."

He tells Sean he and his wife only have a small flat and he finds it hard staying indoors. He likes to be in the open air. That's why he spends a lot of his time by the river, or on the ferry, when he's not working. He has a job as a building labourer on some new houses being built in Wallasey but he is finding it hard keeping that going and visiting his wife in the hospital in Liverpool.

"Peggie's her name..."

"That's a nice name, Mister Driscoll..."

As the ferry comes alongside, Driscoll stares listlessly at the other passengers who are preparing to disembark. He is remaining aboard. Going back over to Liverpool to visit his wife at the hospital. It will be visiting time by then, he says. Or, maybe, he will have to stay aboard for one more trip after that. He will have to see.

"Take care, then, Mister Driscoll." Sean offers his companion his hand.

Mister Driscoll ducks instinctively, as if Sean has swung a blow at his head.

"You wha' ?"

"I hope things go as well as possible... with Peggie."

Driscoll shakes Sean's hand. Smiles sadly.

"You are alright! You! You're still young. You'll be alright... Al-right."

Sean leaves the ferry and walks to his digs along the promenade between Seacombe and New Brighton. His problems seem less overwhelming when compared to Mister Driscoll's.

Chapter 37

When Sean gets back to the digs he discovers that, while he has been in London, Owain and Kevin have decided to move to new digs in Toxteth. They are fed up with their landlord, Charlie, and they want to live nearer the College in Liverpool. There are enough rooms available for all of them to move to the house in Toxteth. Sean agrees to join them hoping it will help him get over the break-up with Catrin and also because he will be nearer Bernadette in the Nurse's Residence.

Owain and Kevin sympathise with Sean over Catrin, knowing how involved he had been with her. It is Owain who suggests the encounter group to Sean, thinking it could help him work on his relationships. Kevin is keen and Nia has agreed to drive over from Bala too, on Thursday evenings, to join in. Feeling there will be strength in numbers Sean agrees to join them.

The leader of the encounter group, Don, is an accountant in the daytime and has led dozens of previous encounter groups.

During the second session, Don asks the group members to squat in an inward-facing circle. Don squats in the middle. He tells them this is an exercise about silence. They sit in silence, experiencing silence together. Sean is aware that his stomach is rumbling. He hears other people's stomachs rumbling. He looks around, grinning, thinking the others will find it funny. The other group members sit stoically waiting for further instructions from Don. Sean stops grinning. He too waits for further instructions from Don. He gradually realizes it is a moving experience sitting with other people, most of whom he has met only the previous week, without speaking; sharing being together without having to make small talk, though he soon becomes preoccupied about who will eventually break the silence and when they will do it. Or will it depend on Don telling them the time has come for them to stop?

The silence begins to assume a power all its own. It says to Sean that only serious, deeply significant observations, are worthy of utterance and anything which is said must somehow chime with everyone in the group. He begins to feel that the group might turn on any member whose words do not meet these twin requirements.

He is sitting opposite Owain. He can see his eyes twinkling with good humour but Owain shows no sign that he is about to speak.

Sean begins to find the silence oppressive but he feels he should leave it to someone cleverer or more experienced in groups to speak first. He would probably say something naff which would be received in total silence. He fears he might come out with stuff about himself which nobody would want to hear. He decides to keep stum. He will let someone else speak first.

Silence. Followed by more silence.

Sean cannot hold back. He starts speaking. Very quietly at first, in the hope that he will not antagonize anyone.

"I feel I should say something... It's just that... Not that I think I, any more than anyone else... should... What I am trying to say is... I find this silence difficult. I am just wondering whether anybody else shares that feeling?"

Nobody moves. Don's eyes swivel, taking in the reaction of each of the group members.

Sean speaks a little louder.

"It just seems selfish sitting here thinking my own thoughts, when there are other people around... Who could, perhaps... It's just that I cannot encompass everyone's feelings, in what I say... Nor can I sublimate myself enough to..."

Sean hears voices which he does not recognize, mumbling to his right. Don lifts his hand in a gesture which means, 'Give him a chance.'

Sean looks mutely for some help from Nia. She is not looking in his direction and seems not to have heard what Sean has said anyway. She is looking gratefully at Owain who has just reached behind him and grabbed a huge bean bag to make himself and Nia more comfortable. Owain leans back, eyes now closed, his fingers laced together over his belly.

Sean looks toward Don, the group leader. Don nods.

Sean still feels someone has to speak. Reach out. They cannot sit there all day. What would be the point? He continues.

"I mean, we are all here, together. In the same room... I just feel we should try to make being here mean something... For all of us... Somehow..."

Silence descends again. Several minutes pass.

A girl called Amanda shifts uncomfortably. Her kaftan is pulling tightly over her knees. She tugs more material free from underneath her bottom, so she can squat more comfortably. Then she speaks.

"I just want the group to know... I feel sad."

More silence. A minute. Two minutes. Amanda speaks again.

"I just wanted the group to know that."

She looks at Don. Don nods.

A long time passes.

The group is either accepting that Amanda is feeling sad or has taken no notice. Nobody comments. Sean guesses at least some others in the group are thinking about the fact that Amanda feels sad. They are with her in spirit, as it were. Those who are thinking about her are probably wondering what, if anything, someone should do about Amanda's sadness. Don is their leader. On second thoughts, Sean remembers, he is the group's facilitator. His role is to help the group understand its own ongoing interaction, as it unravels. The trouble is, Amanda came to the group alone unlike most of the other people. So there is no obvious candidate on hand to support her. Sean wonders if Amanda would welcome his help, if he offered it. He fears that she may already have her eye on one person or another whom she would like help from. Not necessarily him. He may not be seen as the person with the skills to help. Amanda keeps staring at a point on the floor about two feet to Don's left. Don glances at the same point on the floor and then at the clock on the wall.

"Anyone else?"

Sean has a suspicion Don is following a strict timetable worked out before the group starts. Ten minutes for the silence bit. Fifteen at most. Then a few minutes for inputs. Then the exercise.

"Anyone else?" Don says again. Clearly conveying he does not want the group to remain silent too long at this stage.

"Yes..." Nia says calmly. "Me..."

"O.K...." Don looks impassive.

"Since the last session, Owain and I have discovered we are going to have a baby."

A polite murmur of approval and congratulation ripples through the whole group.

"Hey!" Don nods twice this time, as if to mark the significance of Nia's contribution.

"We thought the group should know..."

Sean is amazed. His best friends are expecting a baby and they tell the group before telling him.

Ashamed at how small-minded his reaction has been, Sean rises quickly to his feet, to hug and kiss Nia and Owain.

"O.K.... so, let's..." Don is clearly ready to move on. Last week he had mentioned they would try some trust exercises this week. He starts dragging some sponge mats into the middle of the circle.

"Just a minute..." A man called Philip puts his hand up.

"Yeah?" Don carries on piling the sponge mats on top of each other.

"Susie and I want the group to know..."

"Yes, we do..." Susie beams broadly.

"Yes, Susie and I just want the group to know that since last week's session - we have paired!"

"Right..." Don responds with a curt nod in the general direction of Philip and Susie, and there is a polite ripple of applause from the group.

"This week – it's trust games." Don looks around the group, letting the idea fully sink in. A resigned groan goes up from every member of the group. Sean feels his stomach turn over.

"O.K. with everyone?" Don asks.

A few weak 'yesses' are taken as assent on the part of the whole group. Don nods. Then pauses.

"You look a bit heavy, this week..." He is looking directly at Sean.

"Me?"

"The way you are sitting. Drooping your shoulders a bit...?"

Sean immediately sits up straight.

"So how about being the first subject in our trust game, Sean? It'll give you a lift..."

"Well, I..." Sean is at a loss to come up with a reason not to do it.

"Go on, Sean," Owain calls out encouragingly.

Sean cannot back out.

"I'll do it!" He gets to his feet.

Don tells him to get straight back down and lie flat on his back on a sponge mat. Sean is conscious of being studied closely by the group members. All glad they are not the subject of the trust game.

"O.K.... six volunteers?"

As Don speaks, Susie gets quietly to her feet and leaves the room. Philip goes as if to follow her.

"No..." Don says, "Let her go. Give her space..."

Philip reluctantly sits back down.

"O.K.... we'll need just a few more volunteers and that'll make six..."

Don is pleased with them, Sean can see. He guesses Don has had difficulty getting volunteers involved in some of the groups he has run.

"Amanda...? That's excellent. Well done. That's the sixth we needed."

Don has lined up three of the volunteers on one side of Sean's body and two on the other side. He places Amanda to the left of Sean's head.

Sean notices Philip has stopped paying attention. He is whimpering quietly to himself, hugging a beanbag which he and Susie had been sitting on before Susie withdrew from the group.

"I can't imagine what's happened to her... where can Susie have gone?"

"Take some time out, boy," Owain advises Philip.

"Yes, I need to know she's alright... She has become so important to me, since we paired."

Sean thinks he knows how Philip must be feeling, having lost someone himself so recently. He feels angry at Don for intervening to stop Philip leaving the group when all he wanted to do was to follow Susie.

Don has met this situation before. He simply ignores Philip, who sits cuddling the beanbag, and addresses the six volunteers. He warns them that the aim of the exercise is to lift Sean into the air at arm's length, directly above their heads, without dropping him.

"Sean... you just relax and enjoy the experience," Don touches Sean's forearm in the way he has already taught them during session one, when explaining how important touch is if they want to connect with people.

"That's it, volunteers! On your knees to start with. Arms right underneath him. That's it, Amanda... Support his head. And all lift him... gently now, to shoulder height."

Sean closes his eyes. It reminds him how being lifted bodily felt as a child.

Sean is unable to see him but Philip still seems to be badly affected by the separation from Susie. He can hear him saying that Susie means everything to him. That he hates letting her out of his sight for even a minute.

Don tells the volunteers to bind together even more tightly and they will be able to lift the weight of Sean's body up, all the way, without difficulty.

"Now, grab him firmly, and all together... lift!"

Up Sean goes, instantly conscious of the weakness of the arms beneath him yet grateful that the group members are straining every nerve and sinew to keep him aloft. Their arms are wobbling and, in some cases, trembling, but Don knows that the longer the exercise lasts the more trust Sean will place in the group and the more the group will realize how hard they have to work together to prevent Sean falling.

"Good... good... That's ten seconds already!"

Don is watching the second hand on the wall-clock.

"At last," Philip yelps, passionately. He has spotted Susie re-entering the room as unobtrusively as she left it. "Oh...! Thank God!" Philip grasps Susie's hand and pulls her down beside him onto their bean bag.

At the sudden sound of Philip's passionate yelp several of the group members supporting Sean half-turn their bodies to see what is happening. The balance of their hands is disrupted and Sean's framework of support disintegrates. Some of the volunteers desperately retain their grip but others let go altogether and Sean's body finally comes to rest in an untidy heap on the sponge mat.

Don smiles broadly to cover up his worry that he may face an insurance claim from Sean.

"No broken bones, Sean?... Good... good."

Sean's dignity has been bruised but overall he has enjoyed being the centre of things and feels stimulated by the experience. He gives a brave thumbs up to Don. Don continues.

"O.K. group.... can you all squat in a circle again, please?" Don has decided he has no alternative but to work with the other issue which keeps coming up.

"So, Philip's been feeling very protective. You have a kind heart, Philip. Are you back with us now, Susie? For the remainder of the session?"

"Yes... why?"

"Philip was upset when you left the room. He wanted to follow you to see why you left the group. Only if you want to share with us... Was there anything, er... wrong?"

To everyone's surprise, Susie laughs abruptly.

"I needed the loo. That was all. I didn't want to disturb the group by telling you all where I was going. I'm fine now, thanks."

"Thanks for sharing with the group, Susie. And Philip, hey... thanks for sharing your feelings, too. Better out than in."

Don's next decision. No more trust games, at least for the time being.

Sean just hopes someone else will speak. He feels he has done his bit. There is an uncertain atmosphere in the air.

Amanda rises to her feet and walks towards Sean. He notices beneath the hem of her kaftan she is wearing little golden slippers. Amanda nestles on the floor beside him. Places the palm of her right hand on Sean's left shoulder.

"How are you feeling now?" she asks.

Sean puts his right hand over Amanda's right hand.

"I'm just fine," he smiles. Why he says 'just fine', instead of 'fine', he does not know.

Amanda gets back to her feet. Steps lightly to her original place. Settles herself down again as gracefully as a cat after a saucer of milk.

"Thank you, Amanda..." Sean says, ... "I really appreciate you asking."

Don decides it is time to move the sponge mats out of the way and begins stacking them in the corner. Sean looks at Amanda across the expanse of threadbare carpet which adorns the floor of the room. He reflects that he would not have known that Amanda thought about him after his tumble if she had not asked.

Don resumes his position at the centre of the circle. He stares at the ceiling to signal that he is open to any further contributions which group members may wish to make.

Amanda coughs. Don looks at her. She indicates she wants to speak again. Don nods.

"I would like to tell the group that I don't feel sad any more. I just feel I am here, and that is all that matters at the moment."

"O.K.... Thanks, Amanda..."

"I just wanted the group to know that."

Sean grapples with the possibility of standing up, shaking Amanda's hand and telling her he is glad she is not feeling sad any more, but feels it would be a bit obvious, a bit silly. Amanda has only just walked across the room to him, and then gone back to her place.

And then the decision is taken for him.

"Well, that's it, everybody. Time's up... See you all next week." Don has kept his eye closely on the clock throughout, to ensure the group kept to the time boundaries. He grabs his safari jacket from a hook behind the door, then pauses stroking his moustache.

"Oh, yes... and next week, how about we go for a pint after the group finishes... if everyone wants to...?"

The group members look enthusiastic and Don bids them farewell with a peace sign.

With Don gone the group members relax and start chatting about what has just happened during the group and how they feel about it all. Then the cleaners arrive and ask them to leave.

Owain, Nia, Kevin and Sean go on for a drink afterwards, in The Swan, to celebrate Nia's pregnancy. Owain and Nia have decided they are going to marry in a little chapel just outside Bala.

Chapter 38

The next weekend Sean feels the need for a break at his parents' home in Cardiff. On his way back to Liverpool he gets stranded outside Shrewsbury near a pub called Broadlands. It is lunchtime.

Over a few pints Sean gets chatting to another hitch-hiker called Jim who works as a roustabout on an oil rig. Jim's aunt has left him a cottage on the Llyn Peninsula, which is where he is headed. He tells Sean about his life on the oil rigs. It is getting late when they leave the pub. Two of them are hitching now which cuts their chances of getting a lift. Sean goes back to the pub. He telephones Bernadette who is in Llangollen, staying at her parents' home for the weekend. She offers to drive over to pick Sean and Jim up in her father's car.

Bernadette drops Jim off just outside Llangollen and she and Sean then drive into the town. Bernadette parks the car near the bridge. Sean wants to walk in the fresh air to sober up before calling in at Bernadette's home.

It is a bright, freezing, December day. They walk past The Chain Bridge Hotel, on the strip of land between the quiet waters of the Llangollen canal and the gushing River Dee. Dyfrdwy, as Owain has taught Sean to call the river. Sean is keen to plunge straight into the river to clear his head. Bernadette says it will be safer at a place called The Horseshoe Falls, a little further upstream. They walk on to the lock-gate where there is a weir and water from the river is diverted to form the canal.

"This is the place, Sean."

The surface of the water above the weir is decorated with decaying leaves and twigs and resembles a slow-moving pane of stained glass which shatters as it passes over the curving shape of the weir's lip and crashes down its far side.

Bernadette sits on the river bank in her sheepskin coat and alpaca scarf, under an ancient oak tree. Sean leaves his things at the foot of the tree and wades into the water. He thinks about Pop Connolly's stories of swimming in the River Barrow in Ireland. The sun was always warm in those stories. The water here is icy but Sean is in now and swimming and glad of the dazzling winter sunshine which lifts his spirits. He heads for the middle of the river where there is a rock which forms a shelf where he can sit and rest, the air drying his skin as he stares into the frothing turmoil of the weir below him.

Sean can feel his head clearing. His body, too, is glowing all over now as if he has been sitting in a warm bath. He wishes Bernadette had plunged into the water with him so that their limbs could have been entwined in the cool, cleansing water and they could have sat together on the rock sharing this moment; in their ears the sound of the waters rushing down the weir in a continuous wave, and the hills all around them.

Sean's teeth begin to chatter. He swims back to the bank suddenly noticing the cold is causing his arms to feel numb. Bernadette laughs at his haste and begins to dry him with her scarf.

"Don't look, don't look," Sean implores, suddenly conscious of his nakedness and Bernadette's high moral standards.

"Don't be silly, Sean. There's no need to be ashamed of your body. You've got your underpants on!"

Reassured, Sean jumps up and down on the spot, to warm up. Gets dressed. Runs with Bernadette to the car.

As Bernadette drives them to her parents' house to eat, they cannot stop talking about anything and everything and, for the first time Sean recognizes just how easily their conversation flows.

"I feel I can really talk to you, Bernadette..."

"Me, too. I wish we could spend more time together, though..."

They decide it would be a good idea to go on holiday together, somewhere. Anywhere, really. Just for a weekend. Before the end of term. Sean finds it almost a frightening thought. Bernadette and he have known each other for so long. Since childhood. They are older now. Still seeing the child in the other. Their relationship will change. But it will be exciting, he thinks. Another dimension. A deeper understanding and closeness will grow. They decide their holiday will be a weekend in Llandudno.

Every day, until they go away on their holiday, Sean thinks about how his life is going to change, knowing himself so much better now than he did; he will be true to himself and his feelings for Bernadette, and, just as night follows day, their love will grow.

Chapter 39

Sean feels in his bones that their holiday in Llandudno will be the start of something big. He is half-expecting a little speech from Bernadette on their first evening, letting him know that she feels their days of childhood innocence are behind them and that she is ready to move into a new adult phase of their relationship.

To some extent, he expects it will make them sad. Letting go of the simple innocence of their childhood. Yet he is sure they will both be excited at the prospect of adult love, committing to each other in the absence of marriage which he feels neither of them are yet ready for.

He has been inspired by a book, Sons and Lovers, which he has read from cover to cover in two days after coming across it in a secondhand book shop in Liverpool. Without making any assumptions about the Llandudno weekend itself, the book has raised his awareness of how other people feel above love-making. He reads and rereads the encounter between Paul and Miriam.

'...They went back to the house, hand-in-hand, in silence... He locked the door, and they had the little house to themselves. He never forgot seeing her as she lay on the bed, when he was unfastening his collar. First he saw only her beauty, and was blind with it. She had the most beautiful body he had ever imagined. He stood unable to move or speak, looking at her, his face half-smiling with wonder. And then he wanted her, but as he went forward to her, her hands lifted in a little pleading movement, and he looked at her face, and stopped. Her big brown eyes were watching him, still and resigned and loving; she lay as if she had given herself up to sacrifice; there was her body for him; but the look at the back of her eyes, like a creature awaiting immolation, arrested him, and all his blood fell back.

"You are sure you want me?" he asked, as if a cold shadow had come over him.

"Yes, quite sure."

She was very quiet, very calm. She only realized that she was doing something for him. He could hardly bear it. She lay to be sacrificed for him because she loved him so much. And he had to sacrifice her. For a second, he wished he were sexless or dead. Then he shut his eyes again to her, and his blood beat back again.

And afterwards he loved her - loved her to the last fibre of his being. He loved her. But he wanted, somehow, to cry. There was something he could not bear for her sake. He stayed with her till quite late at night. As he rode home he felt that he was finally initiated. He was a youth no longer. But why had he the dull pain in his soul? Why did the thought of death, the after-life, seem so sweet and consoling?'

The description of the love Paul and Miriam feel for each other in Sons and Lovers takes Sean's breath away; the emotional power of it; even though, sadly, Paul finds loving Miriam out of wedlock, and his mother's jealousy of Miriam, creates a block within him. Sean unearths a dog-eared copy of Lady Chatterley's Lover in the same shop and discovers passion more equally experienced.

'In the short summer night she learned so much. She would have thought a woman would have died of shame. Instead of which, the shame died. Shame, which is fear: the deep organic shame, the old, physical fear which crouches in the bodily roots of all of us, and can only be chased away by the sensual fire, at last it was roused up and routed by the phallic hunt of the man, and she came to the very heart of the jungle of herself. She felt, now, she had come to the real bed-rock of her nature, and was essentially shameless. She was her sensual self, naked and unashamed. She felt a triumph, almost a vainglory. So! That was how it was! That was life! That was how oneself really was! There was nothing left to disguise or be ashamed of. She shared her ultimate nakedness with a man, another being.

And what a reckless devil the man was! Really like a devil! One had to be strong to bear him. But it took some getting at, the core of the physical jungle, the last and deepest of organic shame. The phallos alone could explore it. And how he had pressed in on her!'

Bernadette is waiting for him on the steps of the nurses' accommodation in Liverpool, a small overnight case under her arm. She is wearing a skin-tight, cream trouser suit and her Hush Puppy boots.

"I've booked the hotel, Sean."

"Wow, great!"

"Well, it's a big guest house, actually. In its own grounds..."

"Sounds fine to me..."

Bernadette and Sean embrace warmly.

"And something to relax us, tonight..."

Bernadette shows Sean a bottle of Mateus Rose nestling in her case.

"You… are... brilliant, Bernadette..."

Sean spots Bernadette's parents' car in the car park. The Mercedes. Clever, he thinks. No need for public transport.

Just then Bernadette's parents come out of the nurses' home smiling broadly.

"Wonder-ful... Sean. What a wonder-ful idea. Thank you, so much."

Mrs. Schwackenberg wraps Sean tightly in her arms.

Sean is not sure whether Mrs. Schwackenberg is thanking him because he is taking Bernadette on a holiday to Llandudno, or because she and Mr. Schwackenberg are coming with them.

He soon finds out. Mr. Schwackenberg slaps him on the shoulder.

"So now we see Llan-dudno - together. Yes! Very good, Sean."

Sean is very surprised but if Bernadette wants to have her parents along why should he object? And it would be hard for Bernadette's parents to understand if he backed out now.

He climbs into the back of the Mercedes alongside Mrs. Schwackenberg. Bernadette engages first gear and prepares to pull away but Mrs. Schwackenberg suddenly opens her door and jumps out of the car shouting loudly.

"Holy Water! Holy Water! Don't drive off yet…!" She extracts a small ...stic bottle from her handbag which Sean recognizes as coming from one of ...nes to Our Lady, Fatima or Lourdes, and is thought to have protective ... like Miraculous Medals.

...kles the Holy Water over the car's roof, doors, lights, ...rs, and then over the driver, Bernadette.

...n't let us hurt anyone else on the roads, and please ...en...' ...That's the motorists prayer, Sean."

...rg sprinkles water over Sean's head, and over his

right hand so that he can make a sign of the cross with the Holy Water, and then sprinkles herself and Mr. Schwackenberg.

"All right, Bernadette, darling. You can drive off now."

Compared to how badly the weekend could have gone, the weekend goes really well.

The guest house is clean and roomy. Bernadette shares the big family room with her parents. Sean's room is bright and cheerful with lots of daylight from a well-positioned window in the roof. And Bernadette's parents insist on paying for all the accommodation.

The bottle of Mateus Rose goes down well with all of them, and helps them relax on the first evening. The next morning, the drizzle clears completely by two in the afternoon, and they have a stroll together along the promenade before dinner.

On the Sunday, they all attend Holy Mass in the morning, but, later, Sean and Bernadette catch some time on their own, while Mr. and Mrs. Schwackenberg go to church for a second time for the afternoon Benediction service. Sean tells Bernadette he is going up to his bedroom to clean his teeth. He has finished the brushing and is rinsing his mouth with water when he hears light tapping coming from outside his room. Sean opens his door swiftly to find Bernadette, looking mischievous, on the other side.

"May I come in, Sean?" She mouthes the words silently, although there is nobody else on the landing or the stairs.

Sean does not hesitate. He tugs Bernadette inside, and wraps her tightly in his arms.

"I love you, Bernadette... I've always loved you... ever since we played with the frogs by your parents' pond."

Out of the corner of his eye, Sean notices he has left his copy of Lady Chatterley's Lover lying on his bedside table. He slides it under his pillow. The simple understanding between Mellors and Constance when they met is still with him. Constance had taken off her hat and shaken her hair. Mellors had sat down, taking off his shoes and gaiters, and undoing his cord breeches.

Sean and Bernadette are now sitting, together - on the single bed, in this guest house in Llandudno. Each second seems to Sean to last an hour. They have never before been in a bedroom together. Sean can feel Bernadette trembling with excitement through the softness of her cream trouser suit.

They kiss each other passionately for several minutes.

Sean and Bernadette now sit slightly awkwardly on the edge of the bed, their arms around each other's shoulders.

Sean speaks with the urgency and earnestness of a defence barrister making his final speech to an unsympathetic jury.

"I've been reading this book by D. H. Lawrence, Bernadette. Apparently, he believed that sexual love makes people completely human... fulfilled as human beings..."

"Really?"

" Yes, I know you have principles about this, but I was thinking about it other day. How it might deepen our love for each other even further, if we ? I know it's a bit late now. Your parents will probably be back from any minute now... But I could book us into The Adelphi next . I've still got some of my grant left, and I'm sure Owain or e a few pounds, if I ask them. What do you think,

bout it, Sean? I haven't thought about it since it

Before they know it, the weekend is over.

They both say their goodbyes to Mr. and Mrs. Schwackenberg outside the nurses' accommodation.

Bernadette's parents are lovely people. Cheerful. And they adore Bernadette. Probably one of the reasons why she is such a lovable person, Sean reflects.

They shake Sean's hand warmly.

"God bless, Sean... God bless, son."

"Thank you for a lovely weekend, Mr. Schwackenberg... Mrs. Schwackenberg..."

When her parents have left, Bernadette turns towards Sean.

"Come and visit me in the nurses' residence, will you Sean? "

"I will, Bernadette."

"There's a room there for visitors, just inside the front door. Yes, it's quite private there. We can have a good chat...," she lowers her voice and adds shyly, "about you-know-what!"

"Yes, Bernadette. I will. I'll see you soon."

Chapter 40

After the encounter group, Sean starts to receive parcels through the post. There are always home-made greetings cards inside. Sean thinks they may be from Amanda. It turns out Amanda is in her final year at Liverpool College of Art. The cards are originals. Very picturesque. Naïve. Pictures of the docks; the Liver building; the ferries. All constructed by sticking things onto pieces of plywood; buttons, string, bits of plastic, bottle-tops, sweet wrappers, match sticks, pieces of cloth.

There are always messages written in lipstick, charcoal, mascara, seemingly whatever has been nearest to the artist's hand. They say things like, 'THIS IS THE FIRST DAY OF THE REST OF YOUR LIFE!' and are always signed enigmatically 'A'. But there is not really any mystery about where they are coming from. Amanda has told the group she is interested in modern poetry. She tells Sean every word he speaks is a poem; every word anybody speaks, she adds. And she has taken to sharing a bean bag with Sean at the group. He feels happy to have her as a friend, a friend he would not have met without the encounter group.

But when, during one of the group sessions, Sean shares the fact that he is receiving the pictures Amanda denies all knowledge of them. He wonders if she knows about Bernadette from Owain or Nia and he thinks perhaps she is being discreet. How she got hold of the Toxteth address in the first place he has no idea. But he is certain that life never seems to be as straightforward as it should be.

The most recent parcel has caused him most concern. He admires the craftwork which has gone into the making of it but has decided to do nothing about it. There is no address to reply to even if he wanted to. As usual the basic material is plywood. The picture is of a seascape. The sea, green chocolate bar wrappers. The turbulent waves have tissue-paper foam crests and, emerging from between raised cardboard headlands a smooth purple Cadbury's wrapper represents a winding river flowing into the sea from its esturial haven. Squally strips of liquorice pour down over the headlands, from an otherwise cloudless crepe sky. Sean notices the verse written on the back is written in familiar lipstick capitals...

THE SOUND OF RAIN FALLING ON LEAVES,

FIGURES CURVED IN SHADOWS OF SADNESS,

TOUCH OF TEARS - COOL ON EACH CHEEK.

HE IS HEALED, WHO GRIEVES BY THE SPRING

AND STRENGTHENED WHEN WEAK

BY THE GUSH OF A MOUNTAIN STREAM

AS IT HURRIES SHYLY, TO MARRY THE SEA.

The card is signed not with the usual, 'A'. This one bears no inscription but in large purple capitals are the words, I LOVE YOU.

Chapter 41

The visitors' room at the Nurses' residence is spartan. Two chairs. Faded brown wallpaper. A picture of Florence Nightingale tending to wounded troops in the Crimea.

"Please wait here. I'll tell Miss Schwackenberg she has a visitor." The Bursar, a retired Matron, has looked Sean up and down with disapproval. "Mr. Connolly, you said your name was?"

"Yes, thank you."

Sean has managed to borrow money from Owain. He feels the reassuring bulk of his wallet against his heart.

Bernadette looks stunning, and is as soft and yielding as ever in his arms when they embrace.

They make small talk about the trip to Llandudno, and laugh again about Mrs. Schwackenberg's habit of splashing holy water over the car and its occupants whenever the family goes anywhere.

Finally, Sean broaches the subject they have both been conscious of avoiding. He tries to sound casual.

"I was just wondering if you have had time to think about what we talked about at Llandudno, Bernadette? By the way, Owain has loaned me some money if you do fancy a short break in The Adelphi."

Bernadette does not hesitate but she speaks gently.

"Sean, I don't know if you know. I've always been devoted to Our Lady, the Virgin Mary. I've tried to follow her example in every way possible ever since I was a little girl..."

"I see, Bernadette."

"I want to keep myself pure for the man I finally marry, Sean. Can you understand that?"

"I certainly can. I think you've told me before."

"Are you a virgin, Sean?"

Sean fixes his gaze on the picture of Florence Nightingale. Her pallid features. Her expression of compassion. The never-ending row of wounded soldiers relying on her for life itself.

"Yes, Bernadette... I am."

Bernadette clasps Sean's hands in hers.

"That's beautiful, Sean. I always thought of you as someone who respected other people."

"Yes, I do find it easy to respect you, Bernadette."

"But, I am sorry. I am not coming to The Adelphi with you. Listen to me, Sean. I am willing to share my life with you but I am afraid all that Adelphi-business will have to wait until we are married."

Sean starts to worry about what Owain is going to say, when he has to tell him he can have his money back, that he will not be needing the loan. But he knows all that is unimportant.

"Thank you for being straight with me, Bernadette..."

"Thank you, too... for your honesty."

They hug as if to console each other over a problem neither has caused. They accept it is just how things are. An uncertainty has been resolved and something has changed which they will have to adjust to. Then Sean realizes what has changed for him. For the first time, he knows what he wants.

"It is fine and understandable and I respect your decision, Bernadette, but I am really sorry I just do not think I can wait. I cannot play Saint Joseph to your Virgin Mary. I just know I cannot do it."

"I'll always be your friend, Sean."

"Me, too. If ever you need anything and I can help you, just let me know."

They hug. Sean turns away and leaves.

He does not need to look over his shoulder. He can see Bernadette in his mind's eye. He never forgets seeing her standing on the steps of the nurses' residence as they are taking their leave of each other. First he sees only her beauty, and is blind with it. She has the most beautiful body he has ever imagined. Her big sad eyes are watching him, still and resigned and loving him, as he makes his way back to his digs in Toxteth.

Chapter 42

It is the last Sunday before the term ends. Dinner has been eaten. It is very quiet in the digs. Kevin is pulling out all the stops to keep up with his law notes. He knows most of them by heart but goes over them time and again. Since Owain and Nia became engaged Owain spends most of his weekends at Nia's home in Bala. Sean is looking forward to their wedding in February. It will be such a celebration and they are clearly so happy together. Nia has already sorted out the plans for the service and for the reception afterwards. She wants the place settings to include five almonds in a white lace bag, to signify health, wealth, happiness, fertility and longevity. She has read somewhere that it is something they do at Italian weddings, so why not at a Welsh wedding? And her wedding dress? She has it already, in white satin with dozens of tiny white pearls decorating the neckline, and along the sleeves and the hem. She thinks she will be able to get into it alright. She will still only be about three months gone in February.

Sean cannot settle. He wanders upstairs to his bedroom. Flicks through his notes on the law of contract. He has to keep prompting himself. Finds he cannot reel it off like Kevin does. He decides to go downstairs to see if he can cadge a cup of tea out of their new landlord. The one in Toxteth is a lot more

hospitable than Charlie ever was over in New Brighton.

Chapter 43

1969

It was Mrs Schwackenberg who suggested inviting Sean to the party to celebrate the Ruby Anniversary of her marriage to Mr Schwackenberg. Whenever the smell of bread wafts from the kitchen where Mr Schwackenberg is baking for their guesthouse visitors filling the living room with an indefinable aura of yeast and homeliness, Mrs Schwackenberg thinks of her daughter, Bernadette. Peeling vegetables, crocheting or silently praying she returns to thinking of her.

'Such a beautiful girl and so clever... She's going to be a great midwife. I should feel so proud.'

After working on the premature baby unit Bernadette had enrolled on a midwifery course. Her project on the development of the foetus has been chosen by Dr Hahn to be the first chapter of a book he is writing entitled A Handbook Of Pre-Natal Paediatrics for Obstetricians and Paediatricians.

Yet Mrs Schwackenberg had called to Mr Schwackenberg through the open door, "I wonder how Sean is getting along?" They had heard nothing of Sean for a long time and Bernadette has been inexplicably reticent whenever his name is mentioned.

"I wonder. A nice young man. A nice family." Mr Schwackenberg had called back. He did not wish to interfere in Bernadette's life but he readily agreed to Mrs Schwackenberg's suggestion that they invite Sean to the planned celebration at their home.

On her weekends off Bernadette likes to visit home to see the family, to relax, sometimes to study. Dr Hahn has visited and stayed over a few times and has always been the epitome of politeness. He listens with great interest and respect to what Bernadette and her parents have to say about everything discussed, serious and trivial; he makes relevant contributions of his own; he laughs at their jokes and makes humorous remarks too; yet when she visits home alone Bernadette finds herself playing her old records, humming along to Herb Alpert then joining in the words quietly but angrily to herself… "They say this guy, this guy's in love with you…"

When her mother tentatively mentions that she and her father are thinking about inviting Sean to their Ruby Wedding celebration as well as Dr Hahn, whom they have already invited, Bernadette feels an initial surge of excitement followed by a secondary surge of anger and sadness. She feels she and Sean were so close; so close she could almost say she thought they were in love with each other but he had gone and spoiled it all by wanting IT - more than wanting her, tantamount to not wanting her at all; had not been willing to wait. She has no idea how she will feel seeing him again but, she tells herself, there will be plenty of other people here so I can avoid him if it gets too heavy.

Sean has a worse headache than usual as he picks up his Ruby Wedding invitation from the mat at his digs. He is living at the same digs in Toxteth after dropping out of the law course earlier in the year and choosing not to go back to live with his parents. His stomach turns over as he reads the invitation from Mr and Mrs Schwackenberg. He reflects on his year so far. A job as a swimming pool attendant which enables him to pay his rent and to enjoy a few pints after work; he has just happened to overdo it last night because one of his workmates is leaving soon to join the Merchant Navy. He still sees Kevin and Owain, when Owain is at the digs and not staying in Bala with Nia. They are marrying very soon in a Welsh Chapel in Bala called Capel Tegid. Sean's social life is limited. Occasionally he meets up with Amanda from the encounter group who has become a good friend; she tells him about all her latest art works which he is beginning to appreciate. They meet in the Walker Art Gallery from time to time. Sean is teaching her to swim

Sean is still standing in the hallway. He absently strokes the luxurious texture of the Schwackenbergs' invitation card between his fingers. He has thought about Bernadette every day since they stopped seeing each other. He has been free, makes his own decisions and is now a person in his own right. But he cannot forget the almost umbilical connection he and Bernadette had. He knows if he does not act immediately he may not act at all. He picks up the telephone in the hallway and dials. The receiver is picked up and Mr Schwackenberg's voice comes on the line loud and clear.

"Ah, it's Sean. Hello son, how are you? Hang on a minute, I have lots of flour on my hands… Yes, that's better."

"I'm fine, thanks, Mr Schwackenberg. Congratulations to you and Mrs Schwackenberg – I'm just ringing to say I'd love to come to congratulate you in person at your party."

"That's wonderful – we'll look forward to seeing you then."

"Please give my love to Mrs Schwackenberg and Bernadette and the rest of the family…"

"Righto, son. Bye!"

Chapter 44

Sean is expecting to meet a lot of the friends and relatives of the Schwackenbergs but he is reassured by the fact that everybody knows why this party is being thrown and nobody will be mistakenly thinking it is an engagement party for him and Bernadette. He hopes he will be able to spend some time in private with Bernadette and that they will be able to talk. He wants to share how he has been feeling since they last saw each other.

As expected there are a lot of Bernadette's uncles and aunts at the party; many of them remember Sean and seem glad to see him. Auntie Gertrude, Bernadette's favourite aunt, is sporting a multi-pronged gold brooch which becomes entangled in Sean's cardigan when she crushes him to her with an all-embracing bear hug.

Two great friends of Mr and Mrs Schwackenberg, Fred and Florrie, are the guests most feted by Bernadette's parents. They pay tribute to Fred and Florrie's generous hospitality in short emotional speeches about the welcome these friends gave them when they first moved to Llangollen many years ago during the blitz.

Bernadette is dutifully circulating, checking guests' glasses are full, making sure nobody is left on their own. One man looks slightly uncomfortable. He is tall. About thirty five. Good looking. As he approaches people to make polite conversation he often finds they turn away at the last minute as they recgnise somebody they know whom they have yet to greet. He is not too discomfited. He stands with a glass of lager in his hand looking amiably around as if telegraphing his approval of the friendliness being displayed to everybody but him. Bernadette makes sure Dr Hahn is not alone for long and soon introduces him to Uncle Fritz who is known to love talking for hours on end to anybody willing to listen.

Sean spots his chance when he notices Bernadette putting down an empty tray which ten minutes earlier had been loaded with ham sandwiches. Her cheeks are flushed.

"Bernadette!" To his surprise Sean's voice nearly cracks with sudden emotion as he utters the first syllable of Bernadette's name. "Shall we take a stroll in the garden?"

Bernadette pauses and looks him straight in the eye.

"I'm glad you were able to come, Sean. It made Mummy and Daddy really happy."

"And you?"

"I'm not sure yet. Yes, let's stroll."

Bernadette takes Sean's arm and guides him into the coolness of the garden. He is reminded of so many other times he has spent there with Bernadette.

"Bernadette, I don't know how you have been feeling towards me since I last saw you but I would just like you to know I have thought about you every day. In fact I have thought about you every day since we found each other again that day in the Cathedral in Liverpool. I have really missed you."

Standing in the garden Bernadette glances through the French windows into the dining room where she sees her father inside the house smiling and laughing with the party in full swing; the sound of zithers and mandolins and singing rising higher and higher and she watches her father as he moves around the room always looking out for his wife of forty years checking she is happy and enjoying herself; for him the whole room revolves around her.

Bernadette remembers coming home from school for lunch and the secure feeling she had as her father mixed his version of cheese on toast especially for her, mixing cheese, egg and milk before whisking it into a smooth mixture and toasting it until crisp and brown on top. She looks back at Sean.

"I still feel the same, Sean... if we did start to meet up again."

"I wouldn't expect anything else, Bernadette. I have done a lot of thinking since I last saw you. It would be good just to be in touch again. You know your own mind, I realise that, and I was so wrong to try to put any pressure on you. What do you say?"

Bernadette nods and smiles.

"Meet for coffee one day this week?"

"It's a deal."

Back at his digs in Toxteth the next evening, Sean sees Owain and Kevin. Sean is full of happiness. The others comment.

"You look like the cat that got the cream, Sean?" Owain always notices these things.

"Yeah, a right smug grin on your face, mate," Kevin nudges him.

"OK you two. I had a very good day yesterday. I'm friends with Bernadette again. Do you remember we hit a sort of a block and I ended it?"

The others nod.

"Bernadette and I are speaking again!"

"OK you just said that. Well done anyway - the pair of you!" Owain's words are mocking but his eyes have a kind expression in them. "By the way, Nia and I had some good news today. They have confirmed we can have the date we wanted for the wedding! You're both invited and please invite Bernadette too, Sean, if she would like to come with you.

Chapter 45

On the day of Nia and Owain's wedding Sean collects Bernadette from the nurse's accommodation and they drive to the chapel in Bala in a battered Ford Anglia recently bought from Sean's wages as a pool lifeguard.

At first Bernadette had been unsure about attending the wedding as she and Sean had only been for one coffee together at that stage, in the Kardomah in Liverpool, following their reunion at her parents' Ruby wedding party. Moreover, Sean would be the only person whom she knew at an event sure to last for at least three hours. She was worried she'd feel out of place. Sean reminded her she had once seen Nia demonstrating with him in John Lewis's display window during the student action for peace and then she herself remembered seeing Kevin there as well marching up and down outside the store with his placard. Owain had been at the Catholic Chaplaincy Peace Concert some time later but had stayed in the background and Bernadette had not seen him. So Owain was the only one of the three she had not seen but all three had heard lots about Bernadette from Sean himself. They reached an understanding - they would find seats near the back of the chapel during the wedding service.

Many of the families of the bride and groom had farmed in the area for generations and some have come from as far away as Anglesey. Capel Tegid is as full as it has ever been according to somebody sitting nearby. Its fullness adds to a great sense of closeness which lasts throughout the whole day and the Welsh singing nearly blows the rafters off.

Bernadette is aware of Sean's presence squeezed together as they are on a bench near the back of the chapel and she enjoys the feeling of intimacy. There is love in the air. At the front of the chapel Nia and Owain make a lovely couple.

Bernadette still feels something of an outsider being non-Welsh-speaking and having had a rigid Catholic upbringing but, she reflects, Sean is the same. She senses a feeling of oneness with Sean growing inside her but a more powerful feeling grows in her when she observes how Sean repeatedly returns to her during the wedding jollities which follow the service, when it would have been easy for him to drink too much and mix with Owain, Kevin, Nia and their college friends; he behaves as if he respects her, as if she and he are a couple, which on this day they are, and she likes that. Their world is just as full of music, symbols, rituals and spiritual intensity as Owain's and Nia's, she thinks, and, as they leave the chapel and she gazes at the statue of the Reverend Thomas Charles preaching from his plinth near the doorway into the chapel, she feels a oneness with Nia and Owain, with Kevin and with Sean as well as with W. H. Spaull the architect of the chapel, a oneness and a love for all the people who have ever come together to share their common humanity here in this place.

That evening, after raucously seeing Owain and Nia off on their honeymoon with snowstorms of confetti swirling in the air, dozens of empty tin cans tied to and clanking behind the back bumper of their car, yelled improprieties luckily inaudible in the din, and jugs of beer splashed over the roof of the car, Sean and Bernadette are ready to be alone. They decide to visit the nearby lake before heading back to

Liverpool. " 'Llyn Tegid', the lake," Owain had told them before he and Nia had set off. "It's Welsh for 'Lake Bala'. You've got to see it before you go - think of me and Nia when you do…"

The waters of the lake were still as they parked the Ford Anglia and there was a golden sunset with a great peace over the whole place and the hills were mirrored golden in the waters and the calm of the water entered them both as an inner calm and they both cried with happiness as the last remaining ducks paddled past making their way to wherever they would be sleeping that night.

Chapter 46

The rich almost bitter smell of ground coffee always reminds Sean of proposing to Bernadette in the Kardomah, only weeks after being at Nia and Owain's wedding; his memory still has within it the trace of fear that Bernadette may turn him down but ultimately it is a memory of intense overwhelming joy.

Watching Bernadette's expression turn from questioning, in response to his suddenly serious tone of voice, to a brilliant smile as he asked her the question, "Will you marry me?" and she replying with a simple but unquestioning, "Yes, I will, Sean," had been like watching a film in slow motion, he had felt so tense. Bernadette had said yes and had seemed glad he had proposed. He could hardly believe it. They had treated themselves to a plate of cakes served on doilies on a silver cake stand: custard slices, doughnuts, chocolate éclairs, meringues. They had only managed to eat one or two as, like a river suddenly bursting its banks their conversation had turned to ideas about the wedding, where and when and who would be there, and where the reception would be and the honeymoon and Sean was keen to know what sort of ring Bernadette would like. A diamond.

Sean had been saving up, working overtime, looking into jewellers shops in the town centre in the hope that he would need their services after proposing to Bernadette. Waltham's is a small family business where they do not rush you. The mother and daughter run the business and get to know Bernadette and Sean well during their visits after Bernadette had accepted Sean's proposal and they enjoy taking their time finding a ring Bernadette likes. A simple solitaire.

Bernadette's life continues normally, spending the occasional weekend at her parents' home; they are ecstatic about her forthcoming marriage; visiting Sean's parents who are very pleased Sean seems to be settling down and strongly approve of Bernadette and her background as they look forward with great anticipation to the wedding; studying her midwifery in the sunshine on the roof of the nurse's residence; going to work on the maternity ward where she tells Doctor Honey she has become engaged and, noticing a sadness at the back of his eyes as she tells him this news, determining he should be one of the first on the guest list - he has always been so kind. Her life continues normally but transformed by her sense of excitement and hope for the future.

Sean stands on the bank of the swimming pool in his whites making sure nobody drowns. Always two lifeguards on duty at any one time; one to swim to the casualty if necessary and one to help pull the casualty out of the pool before doing resuscitation. The job involves standing for hours on end, day after day, but he buys some wooden Dr Scholl sandals to stop his feet hurting and his inner world has changed so much his thoughts keep him together; he has stopped worrying so much. He finds he can dream about his future with Bernadette and do his job at the same time. To his surprise he also notices himself going over some of the learning of the law he thought he would never be able to remember, a fascinating subject he decides in retrospect, and, when really bored recalls algebraic equations and the various types of triangle he learned about in geometry. Sometimes he diverts himself and the younger swimmers by practicing throwing the lifebelt near them and yanking them to the poolside at high speed or sometimes hauls them in using the ten foot bamboo pole intended to help swimmers in difficulty nearer the bank. The youngsters scream and yell with delight and he wonders what it is like having children of your own.

When he tells Amanda he is engaged, at her next swimming lesson, she radiates happiness for him and manages to do a whole length of front crawl for the first time. She accepts his invitation to the wedding. Sean wonders if the numbers are getting a bit out of hand, Amanda will be the hundredth guest but he is hopeful Bernadette's parents and his own parents, Cecil and Noreen, who have promised to pay for the champagne, will see him and Bernadette alright and he and Bernadette want to share their happiness with as many people as they possibly can.

Chapter 47

Bernadette wants the wedding to be memorable, "It's a once in a lifetime event, Sean. We want to get it right, don't we?"

The obvious place to hold the wedding service is in the Holy Cross Catholic Church, Llangollen. Bernadette's idea is to hold the service in Castell Dinas Bran, a magnificent ruined castle four miles down the valley situated on a thousand foot high hill. The celebration will be seen for miles around and Bernadette and everybody else at the wedding will be both highly visible and able to see the view down the valley towards Llangollen with its beautiful bridge spanning the River Dee.

"I don't think that'll be possible, Bernadette," Sean is desperate to avoid any disagreement but feels he should speak up. "I think the Church forbids marriages anywhere outside church because marriage is a sacrament."

Father John is a newly ordained priest and the Holy Cross Catholic Church Llangollen is his first parish. There is a shortage of priests and he has been placed in charge of a parish straight away. His ordination has taken place after the Second Vatican Council set up by Pope John the 23rd and he supports all the new practices such as celebrating Mass not in the traditional Latin but in English. He is delighted to be marrying two young Catholic people from such staunch Catholic backgrounds.

When Bernadette smiles sweetly at Father John at the end of one of the marriage preparation talks which she and Sean are required to participate in and says, "How would you feel, Father, if our wedding service took place in Castell Dinas Bran?" Father John agrees in an instant.

"It's on quite a high hill, Father, takes about twenty five minutes to walk up there from the nearest parking and there is no building remaining as such," Sean feels he should warn Father John.

Father John is possibly unaware of the precise location of the castle ruins being new to the area or some of the logistical difficulties which could arise, "That's a brilliant idea Bernadette," he beams, "You'll be that much closer to God than you would be in the church.

We can carry a trestle table up with us to use as an altar, Sean, can't we?"

"That's a good idea Father, yes," Sean replies, picturing them all on the top of Dinas Bran, Bernadette's veil swaying in the balmy breeze, a sunny day and the sound of their hymn singing drifting melodiously down the valley

Chapter 48

The view down the valley from Castell Dinas Bran is as stunning as they had hoped and thankfully the weather stays dry.

"Well here we are everybody - most of us anyway," Father John gets the assembled company to gather around his trestle table. "I see a few of us are still making their way up here but we should probably make a start anyway," he glances away down the steep footpath where a few of the older guests are finding it hard going. Cecil and Noreen are helping one of Bernadette's aunts who usually uses a stick and is finding the walk very demanding, and Uncle Fritz is struggling with Auntie Gertrude his arm around her body half-supporting, half-shoving her every step of the way. Some of the male guests discretely go back down to give them all a hand. Father John gives them a thumbs up and mouths, 'Thank you'.

The service passes in a blur for Bernadette and Sean. Father John exudes a spirit of great celebration over these two young people willingly committing to a life together before their families, before their nearest and dearest, and before God seeking His blessings on their future life together.

Sean is standing near the trestle table with his best man, Owain, who has two gold rings purchased in Waltham's of Liverpool safely tucked away in his inside pocket. Then, by prior arrangement, Bernadette appears emerging dramatically through one of the few stone arches still standing. She approaches the trestle table, her right hand resting lightly on her father's left arm. Her appearance is that of a Medieval Princess in a dress of white satin with a sparkly bonnet to which is attached a veil which shrouds her face until presented before the 'altar' whereupon Bernadette pushes aside the veil to meet Sean's star-struck gaze with a frank and loving smile.

They all join together in singing the first hymn loudly and lustily the outdoor setting somehow encouraging a freedom to give full vent to their lungs, so much so that after the second verse Sean, feeling slightly faint, concentrates on breathing deeply and singing more quietly.

The vows are recited tenderly and movingly and there is not a dry eye on the hilltop. Even Father John pulls a large white handkerchief from his pocket and wipes his eyes to enable him to read from the Missal on noticing that Bernadette and Sean when making their vows never take their eyes off each other.

Mr and Mrs Schwackenberg, as a surprise for Bernadette and aware of her devotion to Mary, the Mother of Jesus, have arranged for a friend of theirs with an outstanding soprano voice, currently singing in the Covent Garden chorus, to sing Ave Maria at the end of the Wedding Mass. Her name is Eileen. Eileen sings Ave Maria as a solo at the top of her voice standing on the highest ruined wall she can balance on. The whole congregation is rooted to the spot as her voice soars wonderously, filling the valley with an eerie other-wordly sound as if beamed in from outer space by an invisible as yet undiscovered god.

Chapter 49

Sean drives himself and Bernadette to The Bryn Howel hotel a few miles outside Llangollen, where the reception is to take place.

"What does it feel like being Mrs Bernadette Connolly, Bernadette?"

"Very odd! What does it feel like being married, Sean?"

"Very odd! But I am certain I will get to like it a lot. It feels pretty nice already. Just how odd does it feel being married, Bernadette?"

"It feels like wearing a new pair of shoes… like being in high heels and wanting to change out of high heels into moccasins as soon as you can."

"You looked absolutely beautiful in your wedding dress today by the way, coming through that archway – I didn't really notice your shoes…"

"Thanks, Sean… "

They embrace properly for several minutes, for the first time since becoming man and wife.

"So, have you prepared a speech, Sean?"

"Oh damn, thank you for reminding me!"

A hundred guests is a lot of guests, Sean only fully realises this after lining up and shaking hands with the first thirty or so, honoured though he is that so many people have given of their time to be with them on this, Bernadette's and his, special day. His face begins to ache from smiling all the time and he also discovers his memory of many names in Bernadette's family is poor causing him to resort to greeting some with, "Oh, hello there!" which works well up to a point - so long as he doesn't have to use exactly the same phrase to the next guest in line.

Bernadette is very happy. All the most important people in her life are there. People who have seen her grow up and others she has become close to later in life. She confides in Nia just how much the day of her marriage to Owain had impressed her.

Bernadette's wedding day has proved to be everything she had hoped it would be, added to by the surprise of Eileen's amazing rendition of Ave Maria at the end of the service. The only bad thing to have happened is that Auntie Gertrude has suffered what seems to be an ankle sprain after the strenuous walks up and down the footpath to Castell Dinas Bran. She now has her leg elevated on an extra chair which the Bryn Howel staff have provided and Bernadette has applied a bag of ice provided for her from the hotel kitchen.

Sean's speech is adequate. He had composed it in the car park. The one thing he had forgotten to do in advance. At least he remembers to thank Bernadette's father for his kind comments during which Mr Schwackenberg said he had always regarded Sean as a son, and he remembers to thank all the guests for coming. Most importantly he expresses sincere thanks to Bernadette for agreeing to be his wife describing himself as the luckiest man in the world. In reply to Owain's jokes about his inability to speak Welsh he had tried a few Welsh phrases pronounced so badly it got a good laugh from the assembled company.

The truth is Sean cannot wait to get away on their honeymoon once the meal and the speeches are over, though Bernadette is still savouring conversations with their guests some of whom she had not seen for ages.

Eventually, they get around to changing into their travelling clothes to drive to their honeymoon house in Port Eynon on the Gower Penninsula but they are starving by the time they reach Acrefair about three miles down the road. They park up and buy some fish and chips.

The drive is long and tiring and it is dark. About ten miles before reaching Port Eynon they hear a loud rattling sound coming from the engine. The butterfly bolt holding in place the top of the air filter has fallen off. The bolt is lost but not the filter casing. Bernadette extracts a first aid kit from her suitcase and secures the filter casing with strips of Elastoplast. Only then does Sean begin to fully recognise he has married a wonder woman.

On arrival at their honeymoon house Sean struggles to open the door. There is something wrong with the lock. He wonders if they have come to the right house having only seen pictures of it in a brochure. Bernadette checks the brochure. There is no doubt they are at the right house. They are tired. They recognise they will have to sleep in the car and sort it out in the morning. It is Sean's turn to be practical. He remembers he has a torch in the car's glove compartment and discovers he has been trying to put the key in upside down. They unload their duvet, suitcases, swimming things, and a hundred other packages, leave them in the hallway and flop down on the downstairs sofa before putting the kettle on for a cup of tea.

Once recovered they explore the house and choose the bedroom from which in the morning they will be able to see the sea.

Bernadette has thought in advance how to make the evening as beautiful and memorable as possible. On top of their duvet she drapes a full-length lace negligee.

They decide to shower, taking it in turns. Sean is fleetingly reminded of things he has read in the past but he dismisses it all as inferior, incomparable to this; a million miles away from this. This is real. Bernadette is before him flesh and blood and is looking at him, a mere mortal but a living, feeling mortal who loves her and wants her and she him.

The bathroom has pine panelling which prompts Sean to start singing – Norweigian Wood – a Beatles number. He stops himself.

This is not his experience; it was a Beatle's experience or somebody else's, not his, not his and Bernadette's. This is theirs. This. Here and now. They dry each other standing before the mirror in the bathroom. They hold each other; enjoy the novelty of seeing their bodies close together naked for the first time in the mirror dripping with condensation like tears of joy.

Bernadette puts on her negligee and Sean his pyjamas and they sit side by side on the side of the bed talking over the truly memorable day they have spent together before slipping easily out of their garments and wrapping their arms around each other under their all-encompassing duvet.

Chapter 50

1984

Catrin Rossini never expected to be living in Munich at thirty six years of age.

She loves living in Bavaria; skiing in the Alps, walking in the foothills in summertime, holidaying and swimming in the beautiful Algarve, and with her husband, Wolfgang, and their two boys, travelling widely in Europe throughout the school holidays. Her ear for languages has developed to the extent that as well as her original English and Italian she now speaks five other languages fluently.

She has always kept in touch with her faithful friend, Penny, with whom she used to share the flat in London. They still meet up when Catrin is in London accompanying groups of German tourists and they have a good laugh about the old days when they were young and fancy-free, and they recall how through all the years they lived there they never got to meet the mysterious Mr. Huxley who, according to the postman, lived in the flat downstairs, but did get to meet their husbands; Catrin meeting Wolfgang by chance when he was on business in London and he invited her to dine with him, explaining simply that he was lonely.

For Catrin, being in London, especially in the autumn, reminds her of those heady, youthful days when she and Penny lived in the flat in Hampstead and, in her hotel room late at night when the German tourists have had their last drink and headed for bed, she still finds herself reminiscing. A whiff of aromatic pipe tobacco in the corridor can bring back fond memories of Rupert and his warm, caressing voice which used to turn her knees to water and, as she dons a bathrobe after showering, she slips her feet into a pair of comfortable, well-worn corduroy slippers which Sean presented her with one Christmas many Christmases ago. Her strongest memory is of driving with Sean to a barbeque in the sand dunes outside Cardiff, at Ogmore-On-Sea. It had been chaotic. She was driving the Fiat Cinquecento her father had just bought her. Sean had been such an idiot at times. On the country roads leading to the beach he had pulled back the car's sunroof, stood up like a tank commander, and started singing at the top of his voice, a song she had taught him in Italian, Non Ho L'Eta Per Amarti. He had tried so hard to get the words right. He was hopeless but she had loved him for embracing the language. She had driven like a woman possessed, thankfully without killing anybody, and they had had such fun when they got there. There had been a massive bonfire and sliding down the steepest of steep sand dunes in the dark. Catrin's memory of that evening is always stronger when she is visiting London and as vivid as if Sean is there staying at the hotel with her.

Chapter 51

2013

Sean is sixty two years of age and semi-retired. He has lived in Cardiff for many years. One fine day in August he goes to visit an elderly gentleman who is in hospital having suffered a stroke. The gentleman concerned is a brilliant lawyer who many years ago had helped Sean travel the road of his own career. The lawyer's beautiful wife is there too. They love art and music and people. They are family friends of long standing and knowing many people in common the conversation that day touches on the lives of mutual friends and acquaintances, some still with them, some no longer living.

It turns out the lawyer had carried out some legal business for Catrin Rossini's uncle and aunt many years before and casually, in passing, the lawyer's wife remarks how sad it was that Catrin had died so young, how sad for her family in Bavaria and for her parents. Sean cannot hide the shock he feels. It is as if he has been struck by a thunderbolt. Without thinking deeply about it, for forty five years he has always taken for granted that he and Catrin would meet up again sometime for a coffee in town, in Cardiff, like Catrin had said they would when they parted in 1968. The lawyer's wife and her husband can see Sean is affected. They are very surprised that none of their mutual friends had told him of Catrin's death at the time.

Sean gradually gathers his senses, thinking how typical of him to think of himself rather than enquiring further about Catrin. She had died in Munich, in 1998, from cancer. Catrin's had not been an easy death. The lawyer's wife spares him the details.

Sean's wish would have been to offer her some solace, any solace at all, or at least to be able to say goodbye. This feeling does not leave him as he walks to the car park at the end of his visit to his lawyer friend and his wife. Later that day he drives to Ogmore and walks for two hours in the sand dunes. He wants to be alone. On top of the sadness he feels he cannot rid himself of anger. The year when the Chernobyl nuclear disaster shook the world eludes him but he wonders whether or not Munich was badly polluted by the radiation. There is something in the back of his mind about mountains being badly affected. He knows the sheep in North Wales were monitored for years after the disaster before the general population were allowed to consume lamb from the area. Anger, frustration and powerlessness course through his veins. He could not have prevented Chernobyl from being built;

could not have stopped that accident happening. He forces himself to

recognize that whatever Catrin went through she is now at peace.

Chapter 52

2015

Sean and Bernadette are watching a TV program called Homes Under

The Hammer after breakfast, one bright summer morning in June. The

program is all about people buying houses at auctions and doing them up in

order to sell them on.

Sean and Bernadette no longer have much energy to do their home up

though are proud of their Shaker kitchen, which they had installed along

with new oak laminate flooring some years ago.

Later, Sean walks the six minutes it takes to the Coop shop, to buy a

copy of The Western Mail.

Before lunch Sean and Bernadette head out for their daily walk on a

footpath which takes them through some local woodland. Their time

together is precious now, not only because they love their walks in each

other's company but also because Sean has been diagnosed with prostate

cancer. The doctors describe his cancer as indolent or very slow growing so

it may remain stable or get no worse for ten years or even longer, though it is always possible a more aggressive cancer, as yet undetected, could be present. Sean reassures himself with the thought that he may well pass away from something other than the prostate cancer; peacefully in his sleep, doing a bungee jump with a faulty elastic cord, or from intense excitement on the birth of his great-great-grand-daughter on his hundred and fourth birthday.

After forty six years of marriage, the prostate diagnosis gives an extra poignancy to each day which Sean and Bernadette spend together. They have never felt closer. After getting their relationship back on track at a social gathering arranged by Bernadette's mother they have never looked back. Sean cannot even remember what the party which took place was celebrating, but he has always been glad Mrs. Schwackenberg had insisted that he should be invited. It was there Sean and Bernadette had recognized there was nobody else with whom they felt more at ease and loving, and with whom they had so much in common.

On their walks through the local woodland, depending on the season, Bernadette is on the lookout for Wild Irises, Speedwells, Scarlet Pimpernels, Bluebells, Forget-Me-Nots, Campions, Herb Robert, Thrift and May Blossom and she adores the wildlife; the squirrels, woodpeckers, robins, blackbirds, herons, wagtails, sparrows, kestrels, magpies, goldfinches and, once, a pheasant, the sole survivor of a shoot held on some neighboring land.

Sean recalls what his grandfather, Pop Connolly, often said to him as a child, "Enjoy your childhood days, Sean; they are the best days of your life!" But on that point, wise though he was, Pop Connolly was wrong, Sean thinks – my life has got better and better, the longer I have lived.

Chapter 53

2018

A year has passed since Sean died in late 2017. His prostate cancer finally proved to be more aggressive than anticipated. It has taken Bernadette time to begin to adjust to living on her own. She is just getting around to sorting out the last of Sean's belongings which have lain in the garage, in cardboard boxes, for years.

The first box she opens contains books, novels mostly, and she decides to keep them.

The next box is full of a miscellany of junk. There is a pewter tankard with an inscription, 'For Sean. Christmas 1967. With Love, Catrin.' It is wrapped in crinkly foil, faded gold, perhaps its original wrapping. Ah, bless him, Bernadette thinks. I bet that was from the girlfriend Sean told me about. How touching he kept it all those years.

Beneath some old school photographs she next comes across a hip-flask also bearing an inscription, Amor Vincit Omnia. She is able to translate the Latin because Sean was always saying, Love Conquers All, whenever they had a tiff of any sort. That's where he got that phrase from then, she muses. She decides to polish up both the tankard and the hip-flask and keep them on the mantelpiece in her bedroom.

For some reason, she discovers, Sean had kept several of his school ties, and a Latin Missal with which he used to follow the Catholic Mass when he was a little boy. She puts these in the black sack to transfer to the Sulo bin in the garden later.

There is more. Beneath his ties and the Latin Missal Bernadette comes across a strange creation which she cannot for the life of her fathom. There is a picture of something made from chocolate bar wrappers, tissue paper and what appear to be fossilized strips of liquorice, all adhering in a random fashion onto a single piece of plywood. On the back she notices a short, mystical verse of some sort and the words I Love You, in large purple capital letters. This also goes into the black sack for later transfer to the Sulo bin.

At the very bottom of the box she finds a linen handkerchief, and hiding beneath the handkerchief a colour photograph.

When Bernadette picks up the handkerchief a small, silver ornament falls out. She recognizes it as a Miraculous Medal. She remembers from the time when she and Sean used to go to church how often people would bring these medals back from pilgrimages to Lourdes and Fatima. Conditioned by her childhood at Catholic schools, she would feel uncomfortable throwing away any item of religious devotion which has been blessed by an ordained priest. She cannot throw an image of Mary, Jesus's mother, into the black sack. She pops it into the pewter tankard where it can remain out of sight. Unprompted, into her mind comes a prayer which the nuns taught her at school when she was seven years old. It consists of four phrases. 'Jesus, Mary and Joseph, I give you my heart and my soul. (Repeat) Jesus, Mary and Joseph, I give you my heart and my soul. (Repeat) Jesus, Mary and Joseph, I give you my heart and my soul. (Prayer for a peaceful death) Jesus, Mary and Joseph, assist me in my last agony! Amen.'

The photograph is of a very young woman in a blue and white striped bikini. Bernadette takes in the full brown eyes, glossy black hair, and flawless skin. She is at the beach, her sunglasses pushed above her forehead and a filter tip cigarette in one hand, trying to look more sophisticated than her years. The sun is shining on her tanned body. It could be somewhere abroad, Bernadette thinks, before tossing the photograph into the black sack.

Chapter 54

2020

The ferries still pass to and fro across the river Mersey between Wallasey and Liverpool, though their names have changed. They are now called Snowdrop and Royal Iris, no longer Woodchurch and Overchurch. Another thing which has changed is that it is now tourists from all over the world who take the trips across the water, sightseeing along Liverpool's famous water front, and taking day trips, rather than the ferries being peopled by the office workers who used to promenade on the upper decks in the nineteen sixties in their bowler hats, umbrellas over their arms, reading the morning newspapers. Bernadette would have liked the new names adopted by the ferries, the Snowdrop and the Royal Iris. She would also have remembered that there used to be a ferry called the Royal Daffodil when she was living in the nurses's home in Liverpool. Naming the ferries after flowers would have made her happy, reminding her of her woodland walks checking out flowers and birds with Sean, though she is no longer alive to enjoy them, even though she kept walking for a few months after Sean died.

What has not changed is the movement of the river. Passing as if in slow motion. Moving towards the horizon. Where the river meets the sea. The width of the river is deceptive, near its mouth. The estuary opens up. The sea, like a stilled sea-monster in the distance.

THE END

Printed in Great Britain
by Amazon